# Poison
# Paradise

---

# Hermina Black

**CORONET BOOKS**
Hodder Paperbacks Ltd., London

Copyright © 1971 by Hermina Black
First published by
Hodder and Stoughton Ltd 1971
Coronet edition 1974

Printed in Great Britain
for Coronet Books, Hodder Paperbacks Ltd.,
St Paul's House, Warwick Lane, London, EC4P 4AH,
by Richard Clay (The Chaucer Press), Ltd.,
Bungay, Suffolk.

ISBN 0 340 18608 9

# 1

## I

A sky of incredible blue, across which an occasional white cloud drifted, as though some unseen hand had cast forth an outsize piece of cotton wool. Red earth, broken here and there by twisted pines standing like outposts of a nearby wood, and in the distance two fishing boats with red sails making a new splash of colour against the far horizon line.

The girl whose dreaming eyes had been absorbing the lonely beauty of her surroundings drew a deep satisfied breath.

After three weeks of heavenly drifting from one sunfilled day to another, she still could not quite believe it was true—this escape from the listless unhappiness of illness back to the knowledge of how infinitely worthwhile life and health can be. Heaven knew, though, she had learnt that during her experience with her patients in the wards of the hospital where she had trained and worked until, returning to duty too soon after an attack of Asian 'flu, she went down with pneumonia. The illness had so weakened her that she was told with uncompromising bluntness that unless she obeyed doctor's orders to the letter, worse would befall. She was no longer in fit condition for the rush and tumble of a big, short-staffed hospital, but after a few weeks' rest she would be well advised to look for lighter work—anyhow for the next year.

The result of that was an interview with Matron who had told her with kind determination, "Apparently you have been thoroughly overdoing things. Dr. Merton insists that you should let up for at least six months, and after your convalescence I suggest that you try private nursing for a time." Then in answer to Sanchia's "Oh, Matron, I can't leave the hospital!" Matron continued, "I am not going to let you risk ruining your health. Take my advice and after your convalescence look for a lighter job. When you feel really strong enough to cope with the work here, come to me again, and—we will see. Meanwhile go and consult the head of the Weymouth Agency. She is by way of being an old friend of mine and I shall tell her she will be lucky to have your name on her books. Goodbye, child, and good luck." Matron could be very human on an occasion like this; besides she did not like losing such a splendid and completely vocational nurse as this particular girl.

Much as she hated leaving the hospital, Sanchia knew in her heart how sound the advice was. But she had loved her work at St. Dominic's and the idea of nursing some rich old lady, or a patient of that sort did not appeal to her at all. That was for the future though; just then she had still been feeling too weak to think of the future; suddenly all that mattered was to just get away from things.

But when she finally decided to spend the month of complete rest and recuperation—which, it had been impressed on her, was a must—in the South of France, it had meant deliberately shutting her mind against that other advice which pointed out how much wiser it would be to remain in England and go to some quiet place where she could comfortably vegetate, and at the end of her holiday know that there was still money in the bank. After all, the windfall which had come literally out of the blue, when she won a competition which she

6

had gone into without a thought of it getting her anywhere, would make—the elderly cousin with whom she was staying insisted—'a nice little nest egg'.

But, Sanchia decided that the tomorrow could for once take care of itself. After all, there were not that amount of nurses in a world crying out for them. As Matron had pointed out, she was not likely to find herself at leisure for long, and so when a heaven-sent opportunity like that came to her why not take full advantage of it and grasp the chance to stay at a real luxury hotel; not to have to count the francs, wondering if they would stretch far enough; to buy a few rather expensive clothes. In fact for once in her life have a good look at the way moneyed people lived!

It had suddenly seemed fun to be just a little crazy. And so, shutting her mind against package tours and economy, she had found it possible to make at least one of her dreams come true and spend a whole month in Provence. It was an ambition which she had cherished since she was a small girl, when her half-French grandmother had often told her of her own childhood in her father's home in the Alpes-Maritimes, and nearing the same spot today she had suddenly made up her mind that an afternoon with the sky and the sea and the silence, would be very much more satisfactory than a hot drive in a bus full of chattering tourists, which included a sprinkling of the type of English who—though, goodness knew, Sanchia was no snob—did not make her feel exactly affectionate towards her fellow countrymen and their womenkind, not forgetting their undisciplined juvenile appendages.

Sanchia loved children, but she had a firm belief that discipline makes them more attractive than a too passionate addiction to child psychiatry, and was better for little Georgie or Doreen, than a blind adherence to the 'let-them-do-as-they-like' and 'express themselves' school

7

of advisers. There had been a couple in the bus today who were certainly raising Herod-like instincts in some of their fellow passengers.

Sanchia had asked the conductor if he could possibly pick her up on his return journey if she got off *en route*, and with a Frenchman's natural instinct to indulge the whim of a charming and ornamental young woman, he had assured her it would be no trouble at all—as long as Mademoiselle would be quite sure to be at the bus stop on time. Because it would throw his time schedule out of place and get him into trouble if he were late returning to Nice.

She had assured him she would be waiting punctually, adding blithely, "If I am not there I shall have to walk back!" And so, with the amused conviction that the majority of the party thought her strangely eccentric to wish to remain in the middle of this no-man's-land, she had made her escape, and enjoyed a heavenly few hours of solitude.

Glancing at her wristwatch now, she discovered there was still nearly another hour to spare before she need go to keep her rendezvous with the returning bus. When she started on this mini adventure it had never occurred to her that she would miss her lunch and was only armed against hunger by the bar of chocolate in her handbag. But now a faint suspicion was beginning to dawn that dinner would be rather more welcome than usual this evening.

Anyway, she told herself philosophically, it was good to feel hungry after all those weeks when food had been the last thing she wanted. As for what was likely to happen after this weekend—she would begin to think seriously about that when the time came.

With a contented sigh she relaxed against the boulder behind her and closed her eyes against the slanting sunlight.

# II

She woke with a start, and the echo of the prolonged tooting of a car horn ringing in her ears. It died abruptly, then as, still a little drowsy, she jerked into a sitting position, began again. Sanchia looked at her watch and with an exclamation of dismay scrambled to her feet. Ten minutes past the hour at which she had promised faithfully to be at the bus stop!

It took several more minutes to reach the road, and breathless from her run, she stood watching the tail end of the long white bus disappearing in a cloud of dust.

Starting to run again she pulled herself up abruptly, realising that it was useless to add that folly to the situation.

They must have waited at least ten minutes! How could she have been so stupid! What on earth was she going to do now? In the first place the road was not a main one; twice a week the Cooks tour took this route off the beaten track, because of the sheer beauty of the scenery between here and Grasse. During Sanchia's whole time on the beach only two cars had passed—one of them a farm lorry. In any case hitch-hiking was not a thing which appealed to her, and standing in the middle of the deserted road biting her lips, she was at a complete loss. As far as she could remember the road which the now-vanished bus was taking ran in a straight ribbon for miles, but somewhere on it there were crossroads because she remembered seeing signposts, and that the bus had passed through a village and then turned off into this long stretch which further on ran up through wooded hills.

There was absolutely nothing else for it; she would have to walk until she met someone who could at least direct her. Of course it was out of the question—unless she got a lift—to get back to Nice, but if she reached that village again surely she would find an inn—or some place where she could put up for the night.

Summoning philosophy to her aid again, she thanked heaven that by now she was in good enough condition for even a long walk not to hurt her. And so she started on her enforced trek, and maybe things would have worked out more favourably if she had only noticed the cavity in the road and avoided stepping into it. As it was her foot went over, and before she could stop herself she collapsed in a heap twisting her ankle under her.

For a few moments the pain was so intense that it forced her to remain where she was, before she managed to pick herself up and limp over to the grassy bank nearest to her.

Sinking down on it she regarded her swelling foot ruefully, realising the extent of the damage only too well. With a sprained ankle how on earth would she manage to go on? It was out of the question to attempt to take off her shoe; she knew that she would never get it on again. Determinedly probing the injury she decided without enthusiasm: *At least I haven't broken the darned thing*—which was at best cold comfort; but when, after a little, she ventured to try and stand up a squeak of pain escaped her, and any attempt to walk on appeared quite hopeless.

This is a nice nonsense! she thought with grim humour. I can't sit here on and off for hours, like the frog footman! So what?

With a valiant effort she forced herself to take a few steps. A glance at her watch and another towards the western sky, down which the sun was descending far too rapidly for her comfort, told her that the early, short-lived southern twilight would turn to darkness all too soon. What was she to do? She had not even got anything with which she could bind her injured ankle. Then suddenly a sound which she hardly dared believe was real, reached her. But for the utter stillness of the air she might not have heard it. While she stood straining her ears and staring in the direction from which she had come, the car came in sight—a long, shining, open tourer.

One of the things Sanchia had always considered really undignified was scrounging a lift from a stranger; not only undignified but the height of folly. However, this was no time to be squeamish, and hobbling towards the middle of the road she pulled off her scarf and signalled.

For a minute she thought that the driver was going to ignore her. He drove rapidly past, and had travelled some yards before he slowed down, and backing came to a halt almost directly beside her.

She found herself looking into a pair of handsome, decidedly annoyed grey eyes which appeared unexpectedly light against the deep bronze of their possessor's skin. A second glance told her that the man behind the wheel of the Mercedes Benz was no uniformed chauffeur but obviously the owner of this very luxurious conveyance.

## III

"Yes? What is it?" The short abrupt question was almost barked at her, and the strongly marked black brows above that embarrassingly cold stare drew sharply together.

Sanchia's maternal grandmother had given her a very thorough knowledge of the old lady's native tongue, which until this moment she had always been able to make full use of when the occasion demanded, But now, to her horror, she suddenly found herself at a complete loss for even the most simple French phrase. To her added dismay, she heard herself stammering in English. "I—I beg your pardon, but—if you could give me a—

11

lift, I would be terribly grateful."

He had known at once what her nationality was, but been disinclined to help her.

Scarlet in the face, Sanchia recovered her memory as quickly as she had lost it, and before the driver of the car could speak, continued in French, "I apologise for troubling you, Monsieur, but I have hurt my foot and I must get to some place where I can put up for the night, or find a conveyance to take me back to Nice. If you are going near any village . . ."

There was a moment's further silence while that decidedly daunting stare still rested on her. Then in perfect English, he said,

"I am afraid my own destination is a long way from Nice. But you had better get in and I will find out what help I can be." Leaning over he opened the nearside door.

This was no time to think, or to regret her impulsive action. In any case, she thought, I can't possibly stay here!

With a murmured 'Thank you' she edged her way into the seat beside her far from gracious rescuer, and releasing the brake with obvious impatience he drove rapidly on.

Any gratitude Sanchia felt for this unexpected succour was countered by the knowledge that she was now shut in a rapidly driven car with a complete stranger, in the middle of a particularly lonely part of the Alpes-Maritimes. Which was not exactly comforting knowledge in these days when knights *sans peur et sans reproche* are distressingly out of fashion.

Have I been completely crazy? she wondered. But what else could she have done short of risking being stranded by the roadside all night—or just limping on with a foot that would be bound sooner or later to give out on her. Her companion appeared to be a gentleman, but a cultured voice and an expensive car *could* be the very opposite to safety!

She stole a sidelong glance at him, wishing that he would at least say something. Then 'whistling to keep her spirits up' she decided that anyway she was strong enough to put up a fight if anything unpleasant happened.

Beside her the object of her disturbing speculation was anything but pleased by the situation. This was the first time he had responded to any of those demands for a lift which, with so many students and other tourists doing everything on a shoestring, had become much too frequent. It was not that he was really hard-hearted or discourteous; simply that he didn't believe in encouraging a habit that was full of potential dangers to the young fools who too often depended on help from complete strangers to get from one place to another, and who could quite often make aggressive nuisances of themselves. Anyway, what was this girl doing on her own at this time so far off the beaten track? If she expected him to be chivalrous enough to drive her where she wanted to go, she had, in the vernacular, 'some hope'. If she was merely out for adventure, she had even less!

Meanwhile Sanchia was studying a strong, decidedly grim profile presented to her. Good-looking? Yes—but by no means aggressively handsome. Thick dark hair, closely cropped; just a suggestion of sideboards. A strong nose, a firm mouth above a square-cut jaw that advertised —obstinacy? Or ruthlessness? His English had been without a trace of accent, but somehow he did not look British.

"What the dickens are you doing hitch-hiking alone at this hour?"

The abruptness of the question made her jump, and before she could answer it was followed by an even more impatient,

"Don't you ever read the newspapers?"

13

"Yes," she admitted, "of course I do."

"In that case surely you should have learnt the folly of cadging lifts from strangers? It is not a habit to cultivate."

She flushed, resenting the word 'cadging' enough to defend herself with equal annoyance.

"It isn't a habit. Unfortunately it was a matter of any port in a storm. I have only seen three cars on this road since noon, and the others were going in the opposite direction. I am not hitch-hiking. I had arranged for the bus from Cooks to pick me up on its way back, and—I fell asleep and—missed it. Then I sprained my ankle and..."

"I see. I didn't realise that." He did not quite apologise but his tone had softened. "I am not at all sure of how much help I can be. I have to get home by a certain time, so it is quite impossible to take you on to Nice..."

"I wouldn't expect you to!" she exclaimed. "All I ask is that if you are near any place where you think I could put up, and—telephone my hotel—"

Frowning again, he slowed down. "My road lies in that direction." He pointed. "But there's a little place called Saint Pierre des Montagnes. There is an inn there where you would be all right for tonight. Saint Pierre is one of those places artists delight in but for the present the ordinary run of tourists have missed it—thank heaven! Though the inn is not large, I happen to know there will be a room. Shall I take you there?"

"Oh, thank you—if you will," she said gratefully.

"Good. Then let us go."

The ice seemed to be broken now, and he asked,

"You are on holiday?"

"Yes."

"Your friends will be getting anxious about you."

"I haven't any—I mean, I am on my own. I am staying at the Negresco."

14

If he was surprised, he was too well bred to show it. Somehow Cooks buses and the Negresco didn't match. As though guessing his thoughts she laughed softly. Always afterwards he remembered that sound. She had such a pretty laugh.

He glanced round involuntarily but it was getting darker and in the dimness it was difficult to judge more clearly what she was like.

She said frankly, "I don't belong to the jet set— exactly. I have been doing a once-only luxury vac, just to see," she laughed again, "how the other side live." Now why, she wondered, should she have bothered to explain? Unless—well, he might have made a mistake about a girl staying alone at a luxury hotel. Sanchia had learnt already that young women alone in luxury hotels on the Riviera can belong to the adventuress class.

His brows went up. She had noticed already that those expressive black brows were just a little untidy. But they were the only untidy thing about him. She had opportunity now to note that his light tweed suit was impeccable —and expensive, and that everything about him matched it. She was puzzled. In spite of his perfect English, somehow, he looked more French than British.

"Do you find that amusing?" he asked.

She nodded. "Yes—in a way. But I learnt long ago that it takes all sorts to make a world."

It was his turn to laugh, and hers to appreciate the sound. "Would it be inquisitive to enquire how you have managed to collect that much evidence?" he asked.

She hesitated. Then, "One learns a lot in a big hospital. I'm a nurse." Now why had she told him? The man wasn't asking for credentials, and could hardly be less interested in what she was. Though they were unlikely to cross each other's paths again, she found her rescuer decidedly intriguing.

"So you are enjoying your holiday?"

"I've adored most of it. Provence is even lovelier than I had dreamt it would be."

"Thank you," he acknowledged. "I love it too. You have not been here before, then?"

"No, but I've always longed to come." She hesitated— "You see my mother's mother was born near Grasse. Her name—her maiden name—was Prevost."

"You have relatives about here?" he asked.

"Not any more. I believe that my particular Prevosts have been gone many years."

"Too bad. We turn off here. I will park you at your quarters. Saint Pierre is only a few yards along the road."

She was suddenly sure that he was going out of his way, and exclaimed quickly, "I think that I can manage to get along, if you will just drop me, and direct me. My foot is not as bad as I feared." (It was quite bad enough!)

"I shall do nothing of the kind," he retorted firmly. "Anyhow, I have a message for Madame Blanchard—the proprietress of the inn—which I ought to have delivered this morning. Madame," he explained," is the proprietress of the Veau d'Argent. Before her marriage she was an employee of my aunt's family."

"How nice to have a family." She had not meant to say that, and he found himself repressing the impulse to take a hand off the wheel and touch hers—an impulse that surprised and slightly annoyed him, for he was not the type to react to strange young women.

"Relatives can be mixed blessings, you know," he reminded her.

The road was narrow, and in places the trees met overhead leaving only the brilliance of the car's headlights for illumination. Sanchia had the sudden odd feeling that beyond that ribbon of light a new world was waiting. If her life had depended on it she could not have explained that feeling, and anyhow she was suddenly too tired to try.

Then all at once the hill descended, and reaching the bottom of it they were in the village of Saint Pierre of the Mountains.

It was completely dark now; the moon had not risen, and it was by starlight that she gained her first shadowy impression of a village that appeared to be built round a square, in the centre of which a tall tree spread its branches. A little breeze had risen and blowing across from the mountains, stirred the leaves, making them seem to whisper together. They were approaching a low building from which sudden light streamed out, when a door opened as the car stopped before it. In answer to the driver's short, imperative blast on the horn, a girl came running out.

"*Bonsoir*, Babette. Tell your mother that I want to speak to her."

"*Mais oui, Monsieur Adrian. Tout de suite.*" The girl disappeared and almost immediately her place was taken by a large woman who came hurrying to his side.

"Monsieur Adrian! *Bonsoir*. What can I do for you?"

"Ah, Adele!" He had alighted, and given the landlady his hand, which she shook cordially, saying, "But this is a great pleasure," and then with a note of anxiety, "There is nothing wrong? Madame la Comtesse ... ?"

"No, no. Madame is better. I have brought you a visitor. Can you give this young lady a room for to-night? You are not full up yet?"

"But no, Monsieur. There is plenty of room."

"Good." He turned to Sanchia, "This is Madame Blanchard," and to the landlady, "Mam'selle is staying in Nice, but she unfortunately missed the conveyance which was to have taken her back there, and she has also hurt her foot."

"*Quelle dommage!*" exclaimed Madame, hastening to help Sanchia out of the car. "Come inside, Mademoiselle. You are badly hurt? I hope not."

17

"Not really badly," Sanchia assured, though her foot was far from comfortable when she put it to the ground. "It is only a slight sprain. If I can bandage it it will be better tomorrow."

"Hang on to me," her rescuer advised, and it was with his supporting arm, and Madame on the other side of her that she limped into the inn.

With exclamations of sympathy the landlady guided her into the hallway and as she sank down thankfully into the chair which the girl who had been addressed as Babette drew forward, Madame Blanchard ordered,

"Prepare a room at once for Mademoiselle." Then to Sanchia's companion, "I will see to the foot. It will be quite comfortable tomorrow, Monsieur."

"I'm sure it will," he agreed, and to Sanchia, "You are in good hands now, and no doubt Madame will be able to arrange a way of getting you safely back to Nice. Forgive me if I run away, won't you?"

"Of course—and thank you very much," she replied. "I'm afraid I have been an awful nuisance."

"Not at all. Glad to have been able to help," he replied rather formally. "If Mademoiselle's foot still troubles her, Adele, tomorrow is Dr Driscoll's day for seeing my aunt, and he . . ."

"Ah but no, no, no! I have the remedies!" she interrupted. "I know what to do for the sprain."

"I expect Mademoiselle will be glad of something to eat," he said. "You will see to all that . . ."

"But yes. Certainly."

"Then good night, Mademoiselle." He held out his hand.

Sanchia was conscious of a brief firm clasp, then their hands fell apart and sketching a final gesture of farewell, he went quickly out followed by Madame. But for a few minutes he was still in sight—standing talking to the landlady, his figure silhouetted in the light which streamed from the inn. A tall man—all of six foot she judged, broad-shouldered, slim-hipped and carrying a finely-shaped head with more than just a touch of arrogance.

"*Monsieur Adrian*—!" He had not bothered to tell her the rest of his name, or to ask hers. But why should he? He had done his bit and was hardly to blame if all he wanted now was to get rid of her! Having transferred any responsibility to Madame Blanchard he could drive away—as he was doing now—and forget the whole irritating incident. Meanwhile, here was Sanchia, feeling quite ridiculously deserted and depressed; suddenly realising that she was very tired, that she was hungry, and that her foot hurt.

# 2

## I

Sanchia opened her eyes and lay for a few moments, conscious of a pleasant sound which, as she grew more awake, resolved itself into birdsong.

Where on earth ... ? She sat up abruptly, staring about her, aware now of sunlight filtering through drawn curtains and of the unfamiliarity of her surroundings. Then, fully awake, yesterday's happenings came crowding back, and she realised that she was in the room in the Veau d' Argent where last night she had been very determinedly put to bed by Madame Blanchard after that lady had bandaged her injured ankle, fed her, and finally practically carried her upstairs.

Although it appeared that Madame had been told about her profession, Sanchia might have been quite incapable of knowing what ought to be done. Madame had assured her that she had an infallible remedy for any sprain, and she—Sanchia—was not to worry. Tentatively moving her foot now she could feel hardly a twinge of pain and when she threw back the bedclothes and examined it she found that it was no longer swollen.

Anyhow, last night she had been too tired to argue, and curiously content to allow herself to be treated like a child. Madame had even telephoned her hotel to report that 'Mam'selle March' was safe and would be returning presently.

Coming back from the telephone the landlady had announced, "It's no use making the fuss. I have told them that you are with friends, and will ring again tomorrow."

Well, here was 'tomorrow', and presently arrangements would have to be made. Meanwhile Sanchia realised thankfully how lucky she had been. The unknown 'Monsieur Adrian' had played the good samaritan with a vengeance! Lying back on her pillows she wondered what she would have done without him. And he had been so annoyed at having to pick her up!

Remembering him very clearly, she wondered who he was. Of undoubted importance in this part of the world; Madame Blanchard obviously thought a lot of him. Of course, Sanchia remembered, Madame had been employed by his family before she married. But Sanchia wondered who his family consisted of. Someone whom he had been in a great hurry to get back to? There would be his aunt 'Madame la Comtesse', and surely someone else? A wife who was elegant and beautiful?—she was sure he was the kind of man who would be particularly fastidious where his womenkind were concerned; she judged that he must be nearing, or perhaps just into, the thirties. It was unlikely that he had remained single. After all, he was decidedly attractive—when one got by the rather daunting side which she had first encountered.

But good heavens! why on earth should she waste time speculating about a man who must have forgotten her existence by now?

He had been very kind, though, and she felt that she would have liked to thank him again. That chance was unlikely to come her way; his goodbye had been very definite. Slipping out of bed she put her foot—which Madame had bandaged tightly—to the floor, and discovered to her relief that she was able to walk without more than a slight twinge of pain. Though she was still limping it was easy to get across to the window, and reaching it she drew aside the curtains letting in a flood of sunshine. It was a moment before the picture that sudden brilliance exposed swam clearly into view, and she caught her breath in a little gasp of delight.

Always afterwards she would remember that first impression of Saint Pierre lying surrounded by hills in the bright light of the summer's day.

Directly beneath her window there was only a striped awning which she guessed hid the verandah on this side of the inn. Beyond it the village climbed in scattered groups of flat-roofed houses, some of them seeming to hang among the trees. There was a small square-towered church, and on one side steep stone steps led up to a house which she guessed was the presbytery; while she watched a black-robed priest came down the steps and made his way towards the church.

In these last weeks Sanchia had found delight in many of Provence's exquisite old villages, and it would have been difficult to explain why her heart should be all at once so completely captured by this one. Never had she felt such a sense of peace—of something untouched by time. She thought involuntarily, *Oh! why didn't I know of this place before!*

Her bedroom door opened and a shocked voice exclaimed,

"But Mam'selle, you are not *out of bed!*"

Sanchia turned quickly and found the very pretty daughter of the house staring at her in wide-eyed dismay. "My mother will be horrified!" she informed.

"*Bonjour,* Babette," said Sanchia. "There will be no need for your mother to mind. Thanks to her I am quite able to move about. My foot is much better."

"But that is very good. Only, would it not be better to rest it? If you will go back to bed, and tell me what you would like to eat, I will bring it. The English who come here sometimes like to have a breakfast."

Babette managed the English word charmingly.

"But I prefer just coffee and croissants," Sanchia told her "and if Madame does not mind, I should like to have it downstairs—am I right in guessing that it can be served outside?"

"Oh but certainly. On the verandah, if Mam'selle prefers."

"I should adore it," agreed Sanchia. "In about twenty minutes?"

"But certainly—I will tell *ma mère,* and then return to help you down. There is," said Babette, with evident pride, "a bathroom opposite." She pointed.

"Oh! that's lovely," said Sanchia. "But I can manage without help, thank you."

In a few minutes Madame came up, appearing somehow even larger than she had last night, and a little inclined to scold as she insisted on examining the foot. She was obviously pleased that her ministrations had been successful.

"There will be no need for the doctor I think," she announced. "But you will not be able to walk far yet. Please do not try. Ah! I forget! You do not need to be advised—you have the knowledge—is it not? Monsieur told me last night that you are a nurse."

"Yes. But you have done better than I could have," Sanchia told her, and certainly whatever Madame had used on the sprain had acted like magic.

The landlady smiled knowingly. "I am good at mending. When I was at the château I had many mendings to do—with boys always in what you call the wars! Now, unless you wish me to help you I think it would be unwise for you to get into the bath today. There is a shower—"

Sanchia assured her that she could manage perfectly and was decidedly relieved when she realised she was to be left to perform her own ablutions. She presently went across the small landing.

Shutting herself in the bathroom she was surprised to discover how modern and charming it was—in fact her luxury hotel had offered nothing better. It was some-time afterwards that she realised this rather super plumbing was something the over-landlords of the Inn had insisted on.

As Madame was now convinced that her charge—for whether Sanchia realised it or not, that was how she was considered—preferred to be left to herself, and was cap-able of managing, she only returned to help her down-stairs and guide her outside, where a table covered with a gay coloured cloth was laid on the wide wooden verandah which ran the whole length of the Inn.

"How enchanting!" she exclaimed. "Oh! I didn't realise last night it was quite as lovely as this."

Even more enchanting than she had found it from her bedroom window. The verandah overlooked the square with the great lime tree actually growing in the centre of the road.

A delectable smell of coffee and baking bread made her suddenly realise that she was hungry. Having settled her, Madame was hurrying away when remembering the most important thing Sanchia called her back and asked how soon it would be possible to hire a car or some conveyance to take her back to Nice.

"Today—but, alas! no." Madame shook her head. "But tomorrow—if you do not mind travelling in the van in which Babette's fiancé will take the wine into Nice (it is most lucky, *n'est-ce pas?* that this is the one week in the month in which he always goes there). He will be pleased to take you."

Sanchia's eyes widened with dismay, "Not until to-morrow! But—couldn't I hire something from some-where?"

Madame shook her head. "Unless you telephone to Nice and they send a car—and that, Mam'selle, would be expensive." She added tactfully, "I assure you the Veau d'Argent is *not* expensive."

"It's just that they will be expecting me back," Sanchia told her. "You see, I never dreamed that I would not return last night."

"I told you that I explained, and it is easy for you to telephone from here yourself," said Madame soothingly. "It will be good for the foot, to rest it." Then without further argument she went away, leaving her guest to gaze after her in dismay.

It was true that her enforced stay here, if it was not expensive, was not likely to have any disastrous financial effect; her hotel expenses had been mostly paid in advance before she left England, and she still had a comfortable sum left—in spite of Cousin Emily's dire foreboding. After all, there would be only two days left, since she could not return to Nice until tomorrow.

Her train of thought was interrupted by the sight of Babette, smiling and so very pretty, bringing a tray bearing coffee and lovely hot rolls flanked by golden butter, cherry jam, and a bowl of fruit. A sight that would have been liable to make a far more disgruntled person than Sanchia accept philosophically whatever the gods might send. Could she possibly have been marooned in a more perfect spot, with everyone treating her with such consideration that she might really have been an honoured guest, instead of the unknown quantity she was? Nevertheless she was experienced enough to be sure that if she had not been introduced by anyone as important as 'Monsieur Adrian', arriving, as she had done, with no luggage, Madame might not have been quite so accommodating.

Having arranged the table to her satisfaction, Babette lingered, obviously wanting to chat. When Sanchia remarked again on the beauty of her surroundings the French girl smiled half-apologetically.

"But I fear that Mam'selle would rather not stay," she said. "I am so sorry that it is not possible for my fiancé to take you back to Nice today, but he is needed at the distillery. He takes the wine to the hotels, and if Mam'selle does not object to riding in the van with him, it will be easy."

"Of course I don't mind—I told your mother so. But it is so peaceful here that I wish I could stay longer," Sanchia replied. "Am I your only visitor just now, Babette?"

No, Babette informed, there were a couple of artists, but they went out very early. Next week the Inn's four bedrooms would be fully occupied.

"You spoke about the wine just now," said Sanchia "Are there vineyards near here?"

"But yes, Mam'selle, the Château d'Aureoul wines are famous, did you not know?" Babette sounded quite shocked.

Sanchia shook her head. "I'm afraid I know hardly anything about wine. Are the vineyards near here?"

The French girl told her that the vines were in the valley below the other side of the château, and went on to explain that there had been a bad year after Monsieur le Comte's death. "Everything was so sad," she said, "and went wrong because of bad management. Madame la Comtesse knew nothing then about the management of the estate; the man whom she trusted cheated her. Then there were those bad vintage years. But since Monsieur Adrian came back, and took over the management for Madame la Comtesse, all has gone well again."

Curiosity getting the better of reticence, Sanchia asked, "Monsieur Adrian was away then, at the time of his uncle's death?"

"But yes ... you must understand, Mam'selle, Monsieur

26

le Comte was Monsieur Adrian's uncle by marriage. But Mam'selle doubtless knows..."

"I don't know anything." Sanchia felt the time had come to correct what she guessed to be Babette's impression that she was likely to be acquainted with Monsieur Adrian's affairs. "I only met Monsieur yesterday," she said. "Did you not know that he very kindly came to my rescue?" And when Babette shook her head, not attempting to hide her surprise, she told her what had happened.

"Oh! now I understand," Babette exclaimed. "I thought that you were a friend of Monsieur's. That explains ..." She stopped, adding rather hurriedly, "But Monsieur is charming, is he not? We are so lucky that he did not stay in England."

"He was very kind to me, but I am afraid he must have found me a terrible nuisance." Sanchia could not help smiling as she remembered how very unwilling he had been at the beginning of their acquaintance. "I believe he thought I might be shamming, in order to get a lift," she said frankly.

"There are some strange people who demand that kind of help," the other girl told her. "Mario, my fiancé, has had experience. Monsieur Adrian," she added rather primly, "is not the kind to—pick up young women from the road." Then with a mischievous smile, "Mam'selle was lucky, was she not?"

"Very lucky," Sanchia agreed. "I don't know what I should have done without his help, because I could hardly walk six steps; also the road was very lonely. I should have been really scared if I had to stay there after dark."

"But it is quite romantic!" Babette opened her big brown eyes wide. "It is like a story."

"I am sure he did not think so. He was in a hurry to get home, poor man," said Sanchia. "I expect he wanted his dinner."

"There is a guest at the château," Babette explained.

"But you found Monsieur Adrian charming, did you not?"

"He was very kind," replied Sanchia.

"Ah, but how sad that it was not he who became head of the family. Now, if he had married . . ."

"Then he isn't married?" Sanchia bit her lip, annoyed with herself for encouraging gossip. She reminded herself that Monsieur Adrian's private life was none of her business, and was relieved when an imperative "Babette!" called from inside sent the other girl scuttling away.

Going on with her breakfast she decided that her rescuer was very obviously the local hero, and she was honest enough to admit to herself that it would have been interesting to know more about him. He looked French, but had lived in England and spoke like an Englishman, and he was unmarried; that was probably all she would ever know. But it did not occur to her that it was unusual for her to feel so much interest in a man who was a complete stranger, even if the circumstances excused the interest. She was not the type who wove romances round any attractive male who crossed her path. She had often been twitted by more man-conscious colleagues for being so very down-to-earth over the opposite sex, and sometimes she wondered if she would ever fall in love as so many of the girls she knew did. Not that she was either cold or hard, only that somehow the right person had not come along yet, and she was wise, and particular enough, not to fancy second-best.

Anyhow she had other things than attractive young men to think about now, and as soon as she had finished breakfast she went in search of the telephone. She met Madame Blanchard on the threshold and having been directed to the instrument, began the usual struggle with the operator. Finally she was put through to her hotel and assured them that she would be returning tomorrow; that done she went back to her seat on the verandah.

Babette had cleared the table and left a number of papers and magazines on it; among them was a brochure which on examination turned out to be a potted guide to the neighbourhood. Seizing on it, Sanchia scanned the printed pages and learnt from them that for hundreds of years Saint Pierre des Montagnes and all the land surrounding it had been the property of the Comtes d'Aureoul, and that the château wines were famous, as some of the best of the Provence vineyards. The château itself had descended from father to son from generation to generation, unbroken by wars, the revolution, and various other disturbances, but with the death of the late Comte in the middle sixties of this century, the title had died out, the only son having been killed in the second war. After that there was no further mention of the family; the guide merely continuing with desscriptions of the scenery and the names of famous artists who had stayed at the Inn, and a reference to Jean Blanchard's cooking which was apparently famous throughout that part of the country.

So there was no Comte d'Aureoul now and Adrian was only the Comtesse's nephew!

## II

Presently, beginning to feel rather at a loose end, Sanchia decided to go for a stroll. Still limping a little, she made her way in the direction of the orchard which lay on the other side of the house; beyond it she could glimpse a farmyard where hens and geese ran freely, and ducks swam on a small pond.

Leaning over a white gate she watched the poultry dreamily. In such a short time now this would be only a shadowy interlude. She wondered where she would be this time next week.

She had loved her work at the hospital and the idea

of not going back was becoming more and more depressing. Matron had assured her there was no likelihood of her not being able to get work. Of course she would put her name down at that agency, but what kind of cases was she likely to get? She still did not exactly fancy nursing rich patients!

Oh well! she decided rather ruefully, it's no use worrying.

But however much she was inclined to laugh at herself, she knew that when she went she would leave a slice of her heart here in Saint Pierre. What was it about the place that seemed to weld her to it? Perhaps some kind of atavism; maybe her grandmother had been born in just such a village as this.

"Good morning."

Coming out of her reverie with a startled exclamation, she turned swiftly and found herself looking up into the smiling eyes of the man whom she had been so sure that she would never meet again.

# 3

## I

"Oh! Good morning." She hoped she sounded less breathless than she felt. She really must be out of condition when the least thing sent her heart racing in that uncomfortable way.

Meeting his cool, rather amused look, she felt her colour rising.

"What wonderful daydream did I bring you back from?" he asked.

"None." She was quite calm again now. "At least, I was feeling rather frustrated because I did not know about this heavenly village before."

"You like it?"

"I've completely fallen in love with it."

"How charming of you—I am rather fond of it myself." He had fallen into step beside her as she turned back towards the house. He said, "When I heard that you were staying until tomorrow I wondered if you might not feel trapped, and be cursing me accordingly."

"How ungrateful that would be!" she exclaimed.

"It might be natural—if you were in a hurry to get back," he suggested. "By the way, how's the foot?"

"Much better, thank you. I don't suppose I could walk very far yet, but Madame's liniment has done wonders for me."

"Fine. Though you had better not expect too much

from it." Meeting the smile in his eyes she wondered how she could ever have thought him cold and what a young actress friend of hers would have described as 'up stage'.

"I am glad you are satisfied to stay. Nevertheless I must apologise for not being able to come to the rescue and drive you back to Nice myself," he told her. "Unfortunately we have an important guest, and I cannot possibly be absent for long."

"I wouldn't for a moment have expected you to—do anything like that," Sanchia protested. "Surely once is enough." More at ease now, she added, "But I am glad to have the opportunity to thank you again for coming to my rescue, as you so kindly did." She had not meant to sound so formal, but then—how else could she sound? After all, she hardly knew the man.

Although she was not looking at him she felt sure that those expressive brows were raised again.

"There was no question of being kind," he pointed out coolly. "I could not leave you stranded in the middle of the road, could I?"

Glancing up she met the amusement that replaced that formidably cold annoyance which she remembered. "Well, you know, you could have done," she pointed out, repressing a sudden desire to laugh. "I believe that you would have rather liked to."

"Even if you are right, and that was my momentary instinct, I hope I would never have given way to it."

Sanchia was already regretting her frankness, but to her relief she saw his lips twitching. She said quickly, "Anyhow, you were kind, and I am grateful."

"Then we are both satisfied," he told her. They had reached the verandah and paused by the steps leading up to it. He said abruptly, "You will have to rest that ankle, you know. Come along." Taking her arm without further preamble, he guided her up the shallow steps and across to one of the tables. Nothing could have been more impersonal than his touch, and he released her almost immediately, and yet she was aware again of a curiously breathless disturbance and wondered once more what was wrong with her.

As calmly as though their meeting had been arranged, he drew out a chair from one of the tables and waited for her to take it, asking, "What can I order for you? Coffee?"

"It doesn't seem long since I had breakfast," she confessed. "Honestly, I don't think I want anything."

"But you cannot condemn me to drink alone!" he said firmly. "And anyway, it is a long time since *I* had breakfast. I have been working quite hard for several hours and I really deserve my 'elevenses'—hello! here comes Babette to solve the problem."

"*Bonjour, M'sieur.*" Babette was all smiles as she set down the tray she was carrying. "My mother thought you would need refreshment, and that Mam'selle would join you. It is the '64 vintage." Filling the glasses with sparkling golden wine she informed, "My father hopes you will eat *déjeuner* here. He says that your favourite *daube Béarnaise* is on the menu."

"Then I shall most certainly be here. If Mademoiselle will do me the honour of lunching with me?" he looked interrogatively across at Sanchia.

"That is—very kind of you—thank you." She felt it would be difficult to refuse the invitation—even if she had wanted to, and she was honest enough not to pretend that she did not want to. It would, in fact, be pleasant to spend a little time in the company of this man who was so different from any she had met before.

But as Babette tripped away, Sanchia could not help wondering what the girl was thinking. That the storybook situation which had so obviously appealed to her, was developing? Though it was quite likely that Babette knew

33

that this was only what this relative of Madame la Comtesse—who was apparently also the manager of her estate, felt was due to someone who found themselves marooned in the environs of Madame's property. Especially when he was responsible for her presence there.

Pushing a glass towards her, Adrian said, "I hope you will like the wine Saint Pierre provides, since you are kind enough to be glad to have made his acquaintance. Your very good health, Mam'selle, and may worse never befall you than the adventure that has brought you here."

Would better ever befall her? she wondered, and raising her own glass smiled a little shyly over the brim of it. "Thank you, Monsieur. Your very good health."

He thought involuntarily how charmingly natural she was, and no longer regretted obeying the impulse that had brought him here to further their acquaintance, though he would have been sure—if he had considered the matter—that was the last reason which had prompted it. Anyhow, she was quite a pleasant change, and he could not be more bored than he had been these last few days. There were many worse ways of passing a couple of hours than in the company of a young woman who was easy to look at, and seemed intelligent. She might not be classically beautiful, but that red-brown hair made a pleasing contrast to golden-brown eyes. Yes; on the whole he was satisfied. Or perhaps resigned to the development of his casual act of courtesy. Although put into words his thoughts could have sounded calmly arrogant, that kind of outlook was not characteristic of him; it was more that circumstances had taught him to be self-sufficient.

He said now, in the easy way that she was growing used to, "It is about time we were properly introduced. You probably already know that my name is Adrian Carnforth."

So he must be English! "I didn't know your second name," she told him. It seems that 'Monsieur Adrian' is considered enough to go on with. "I am Sanchia March."

He gave her a little bow which somehow matched his appearance more than it did his name. "How do you do, Miss March. And having got that over, let me proceed to apologise again for having parked you and being unable to drive you back to Nice. But the man who is staying with us is on a business visit, and I can't leave him to my aunt. I was obliged to be absent yesterday, and she had him on her hands to a tiring extent. I am now tied until he leaves on Saturday. My cousin has taken him out today, and as my aunt is resting I have some free time." Time which he had not meant to spend as he was doing; he had not intended to waste more than a very little of it on this errand, yet here he was, committed to give this young woman lunch, and waste his precious hours keeping her amused. Oh well, Blanchard's cooking was always worth sampling, and in a way Adele had let him in for this.

"How much longer will you be in Provence for?" he asked.

"I go back on Saturday."

"And you really don't mind having today filched from you?"

"Not a bit. I told you—I have fallen in love with Saint Pierre," she said frankly. "I don't quite know why, except that it—it seems so away from the rush and bustle the world has become."

"Yes, it is not exactly jet set!" he agreed. "But I understood you were keen to see that other way of life."

"I was."

"Wasn't it as fascinating as you expected?"

"I think it would have been better fun if I had had a friend with me." She gave a little shrug.

"Personally I find big hotels intensely boring," he told her. "In fact I don't like cities."

"I love the country," she admitted. "Especially when it is like this is—so marvellously *peaceful*."

"That depends." There was a touch of dryness in his tone, and then: "Look, there is an hour to spare before Blanchard presents us with his masterpiece, meanwhile I have a perfectly good car doing nothing—permit me the pleasure of showing you something of what you have missed by not becoming acquainted with Saint Pierre of the Mountains before."

Rather startled by his suggestion she said quickly, "That's very kind of you, but—haven't you—that is, wouldn't it be—" she broke off annoyed with herself for not accepting or rejecting his offer at once.

Not appearing to notice her confusion, he rose, saying, "I think a run would be good for you. That is, unless it would bore you ..."

"Indeed it would not. I only wondered if there were not something else you wanted to do," she told him.

"Nothing at all. Let us go."

He had left his car by the front entrance, and having helped her into the seat beside the driver's, he said, "If you will excuse me for a moment ..." Then as Madame Blanchard appeared in the entrance: "Ah! there you are, Adele. I am taking Mademoiselle for a short drive. We will be back in time for *déjeuner*—and with good appetite for Blanchard's cuisine."

"*Oui, Monsieur*. It is good that you are able to show Mam'selle a little of the country." Madame approved. "Madame la Comtesse is well today?"

"Quite well, and resting," he replied. "By the way, would you ring and tell Celeste that I shall not be back until later this afternoon."

"But certainly, M'sieur. I will do that. *Bon voyage*. Take care of Mam'selle."

Sanchia repressed a smile at the odd mixture of respect and familiarity in the landlady's manner, which she already guessed came from having known—and undoubtedly been in a position to scold—him, since he was a small boy.

"I won't decant her on the road," said Adrian, "or lose her on the way."

"Non, non, Mam'selle is safe," smiled Madame, "you are not the careless one." And as he drove off she remained watching until, passing beyond the square the car was hidden by a bend in the road. Then, a smile on her lips, she turned back into the house. Ah, but how kind, that Adrian! she thought with affectionate approval. Even when he was small he had always had a gift for doing the right thing. He was, in fact, a born *grand seigneur*. What a thousand pities that he had not been born a d'Aureoul. Now, if only *he* had been Monsieur le Comte's nephew instead of Madame's! She sighed, shaking her head sadly as she went to make her telephone call.

While Babette, who had been watching from an upper window, was thinking what *grand dommage* it was that Monsieur Adrian and the pretty young English mademoiselle to whose rescue he had come so romantically yesterday, would not have more time to get acquainted. Babette's natural interest in romance was heightened just now by the fact that she was in love and living for the day when she could marry her Mario—which her parents insisted was not to be for another six months. Of course it was natural for Monsieur to have come to enquire about Mam'selle's hurt ankle; and as she was obliged to remain here, show her some courtesy. But how thrilling it would have been if a real romance had developed! Babette had always thought it a pity that Madame la Comtesse's so handsome and charming nephew should have neither fiancée, wife, or *belle amie* in his life. Facts which she had gathered from *her* aunt who was the comtesse's personal maid.

# 4

## I

The last thing in Adrian's mind, while he steered his car adroitly up the corkscrew road which led through the wooded mountains, was romance. He was still far from admitting that the tiresome female whose appeal to his chivalry had so annoyed him yesterday evening had interested him sufficiently to make him want to see her again. Yet now he was aware of her sitting beside him—a curiously restful young woman!

Conscious of the prolonged silence, Sanchia wondered if she ought to break it, or wait until she was spoken to.

Then as they emerged from the dimness of overhanging trees on to a plateau from which the countryside was visible for miles around, an involuntary exclamation escaped her.

"Oh, it is lovely!"

"Yes, it's rather nice," he agreed.

Looking round quickly she could not repress a little gurgle of laughter. He had remembered that sound and it was her laugh that had remained most clearly in his mind. He turned his head, and meeting his enquiring look she found courage to explain,

"I couldn't help laughing, that was such a very English understatement!"

"And it sounded out of the picture?"

Rather pink in the face again, but feeling that frankness was better than trying to evade the issue, she asked, "You are—partly English, are you not?'

"Ah! Babette has been telling you things." Though his eyes were on the road, she saw with relief that he was smiling.

"Why Babette?" she asked.

He did not explain that Madame Blanchard herself would not have dreamed of discussing what she would consider was not a stranger's business. "Babette," he pointed out, "is somewhat restricted and finds great relief in a little harmless chatter."

"She thinks the world of you," Sanchia defended. "Anyhow, all she said was that you had been living in England before you came here and—your name is English, isn't it?"

A momentary frown crossed his face, but he sounded coolly undisturbed as he told her, "To get the record straight, my mother was French; she married an East Anglian squire who owned a—rather lovely estate."

"And that is where your home is! I'm East Anglian too," she told him impulsively. "I felt that your name was familiar. Of course! You must be the owner of Redleigh Hall—" She broke off remembering with dismay that the beautiful old mansion and its acres of land were no longer in the full possession of the family who had owned it since the days of Elizabeth the First— who had probably caused a dent in the family fortunes as long ago as the sixteenth century, when she had made one of her famous, and for her hosts, extremely expensive 'progresses' to their homes.

Beside her Adrian said quietly, "That is where my home was. At present it is in other hands, though I hope that is a temporary arrangement. And so we are fellow East Anglians, Miss March? That would have made it much worse if I had left you stranded."

She had noticed the tightening of his mouth a few

moments back and, certain that he was steering her away from further mention of his more intimate concerns, she said quickly, "I'm afraid I am rather a fraud. The fact is although I was born at Leydon St. Mary, I left there when I was seven—after my father, who was the rector there, died. My mother and I went to live with my grannie (her mother). But we went back very often to stay with my father's brother—he had a house near Newmarket. But he died the same year my mother did, and his sons are now in America."

And, since her grandmother was also dead, she must be quite alone in the world! He frowned, curiously disturbed by the idea. He did not press for further information, but changing the subject again, directed, "Look over to the right, you can see the Château from here."

Her eyes following his pointing finger, she was able to glimpse the house beyond a fringe of trees which would have hidden it if she had not been looking down from this height—a long grey building flanked by those square towers which are a characteristic of many of the old châteaux of Provence. Splashes of bright colour suggested a flowering garden, but though her sight was good it was not possible to get more than a brief impression of what the house was really like.

But it looked smaller than she had expected a house which was so evidently of such great importance to a whole community to be. Beyond it she could just make out what must be acres of brown earth showing between low growing rows of green, which the observations she had made from the plane that had brought her from England, helped her to recognise as what she had discovered with a shock of disappointment at the time, were vines.

"Do you know, I always thought that grapes grew very high up," she confessed. "I pictured them hanging down in great clusters."

41

He smiled. "And you did not find the reality nearly as picturesque as you expected. That's too bad, but you will have to go to Italy or Portugal for that. Anyhow, we don't make a great deal of wine in Provence—you would have to go to Anjou for the big—and great—vintages."

"But I am told that the Château d'Aureoul wine is famous. It is certainly very nice to drink," she said.

Adrian laughed. "That is charmingly polite of you. Perhaps you will try it again at lunch."

"If I don't, it will not be because I don't like it, Mr. Carnforth." She flushed, meeting the amusement in his eyes. She had firmly refused a second glass on the plea that she had never in her life before drunk wine in the morning and dare not risk going to sleep for the rest of the day!—or worse.

It was certainly not that half a glass of light liquid that was responsible for the rise in her spirits which made her feel a sudden new delight in life as she joined in his laughter.

"So you are going back to England in a few days?" he said, starting the car again. "Don't you find your work at the hospital wearing at times?"

"I am not going back to the hospital," she told him.

"You are giving up nursing?"

"Oh no!" And then, without in the least meaning to, she found herself explaining.

"Hard luck if you like hospital work," he said. "But isn't private nursing more—remunerative? When my aunt was ill last year—she suffers from arthritis and she got a particularly bad dose—she was obliged to have a nurse for a time. From what the young woman said she preferred going from one case to another, and seeing different parts of the country. After she left we heard that she married her next case—a wealthy businessman who apparently fell for her ministrations and was determined to make sure of them. My aunt detested her!"

"Oh, I'd hate that—I mean, it would be most uncomfortable to have personal relationships mixed up with a professional one."

"Possibly," he agreed. "I was not suggesting you should look for that kind of job."

She felt a little shock of surprise at the discovery that the decidedly forbidding side of him, which she had first experienced, could reverse quite so completely on further acquaintance, and that she should find herself telling him all this.

There was no doubt about Babette being right when she insisted that Monsieur Adrian was *très charmant*. By the end of their drive Sanchia had no shadow of doubt left on that score; he seemed so unexpectedly easy to know.

Later, sharing the luncheon in which Adrian assured her Monsieur Blanchard had surpassed himself, it needed no wine to make Sanchia feel more relaxed and altogether happier than she had done throughout her holiday. But as the old adage goes,

> Good things and bad things
> and all things get over

and this very good thing had to come to an end. They had found so much to talk about. In answer to her interested questions he had explained the process by which the wine in her glass had been made. Presently she discovered that Adrian had doctor friends in London and, also one particular English doctor here, who was evidently a great friend, and who ran a private hospital nearby which had become known much further afield for the cures for rheumatic complaints which it now specialised in.

"You'd like Driscoll," Adrian said, "and you would have something in common as I understand he was once by way of being a big noise at your hospital—and likely to become a bigger one when he left England to take a partnership in this clinic. It was just a nursing home in those days—not very important then. This was long before your day—and I must have been a schoolboy at the time."

"But I've heard of Dr. Driscoll," exclaimed Sanchia. "We had a preponderance of arthritics in the ward I was on, and Sister—she's getting towards retirement—was always talking about Dr. Driscoll—she said he was one of the real losses to British medicine. He married one of her nurses, didn't he?"

"Yes—she became his Sister-in-Charge,* I believe," Adrian replied. "Theirs is one of those ideal marriages which appear more often in fiction than real life."

"Now why do you say that?" she asked, receiving an unpleasant little shock at his cynical tone. "There are thousands of happy marriages."

"No doubt. But not ideal ones," he retorted. "Don't look so shocked." Suddenly he was thinking that she was very young, and hoping she would not be disillusioned.

At that moment Madame Blanchard came hurrying out of the Inn. Reaching the table where they had lunched under the gaily striped awning on the verandah, she exclaimed, "One thousand pardons, M'sieur Adrian, I do not know what has come to me—I must be growing old and forgetful—"

"What's the matter, Adele?" he asked.

"I should have told you as soon as you came back. Madame la Comtesse asked particularly that you should be back by three o'clock. She said it would be enough if I told you that the papers had arrived, and she would like to discuss them. But I should have remembered at once—"

Adrian glanced down at his wristwatch. "That is all right," he assured her, "there is time yet. You won't go

* See *Sister-in-Charge*.

to the guillotine this time. Let us have our coffee—is it ready?"

"In three minutes," she assured. "You will not keep Madame la Comtesse waiting."

In three minutes the coffee was brought. Drinking it, Sanchia's companion went on talking to her as calmly as though he had all the afternoon to spare, though it was already quarter to three. But the spell of these last hours was broken; she wondered if it could be her imagination, or if her companion had become suddenly a little remote, a trifle more formal. Then, when he had finished his coffee, he rose.

"I am afraid I shall have to say goodbye," he said, holding out his hand. "It has been charming meeting you —I hope you have the best of luck on your return, and meanwhile—*bon voyage.*"

"Thank you very much, Mr. Carnforth, for a lovely lunch, and my drive and—yesterday. Goodbye—" she put her hand into his.

With a brief pressure he released it, sketched a final farewell salute and was gone.

Sanchia had always prided herself on her common sense, and so surely it was more than absurd to feel that same unhappy—almost deserted—feeling, which had come to her in exactly the same circumstances last night. She had been sure then that she would not see him again! This time she was doubly convinced.

Oh well! It had been a delightful break—something to remember with pleasure, but not with such a curious sense of—loss.

And, driving rapidly away, Adrian Carnforth decided that what he had at the beginning considered a necessary but rather boring duty call, had turned out—very pleasantly. She really was refreshingly different from the usual run of young women who had come his way, whose chief aim in life seemed to be a determination to

45

impress their 'sexiness' on every possible—or impossible —male. As a popular, and until a year ago, an apparently rich young man, he had had his full share of feminine attention thrown at him, and grown bored and cynical enough to pity the fools who rushed into marriage and were too often more anxious to rush out of it. Anyhow, it had been pleasant to meet a girl who appeared natural and unselfconscious, and certainly did not seem to think it necessary to play up to one.

Could be her profession that had taught her to put a stopper on the 'come hitherness'. Keen on her work too! He had guessed that from the way she spoke about it. Oh well, he hoped she would find the kind of cases she wanted. Yes, she certainly was rather refreshing. Then reaching his destination he dismissed her from his mind.

## II

Anyway, she had travelled light this time, and there was nothing to pack!

Taking a final look round the bedroom which had been home for these two nights, Sanchia hesitated, then walking across to the open window, stood looking out at the glorious view which she knew instinctively she would always remember with a trace of regret. From where she stood she could see the upward winding road over which she had been driven yesterday. She wondered what Adrian Carnforth was doing today? Going about his own concerns, of course, and whatever those were—apart from his work as manager of the d'Aureoul lands and business— they were nothing to do with her. There could be no point at which their lives were ever likely to touch again. But how odd it was that they should come from the same part of England and each have a link with this other fair land. Under the circumstances it was

46

natural to feel—well, a certain amount of interest in him. Ever since they parted she had found herself remembering the bitterness in his tone when he had spoken of the house which should be his, and how quickly he had turned the conversation. Her natural intuition told her that something must have gone very wrong, and that though he spoke of Saint Pierre with such evident affection, he was not really a willing exile.

But it was characteristic of Sanchia that she had not indulged her curiosity by trying to find out more about him from Babette. If her uncle and cousins had still been in Suffolk she could easily have found out what had happened to Redleigh Hall, but, as she had told Adrian, Uncle James was dead and his sons farming in the U.S.A.

Turning away from what she was convinced was her farewell view of Saint Pierre, she went downstairs. There was half an hour yet before Mario would come to collect her. She wished it could be now, because it really did seem silly to feel so sad at leaving a place which less than two days ago she had never even heard of.

Anyhow, thank goodness her foot was quite better. Did she wish she had never hurt it? That she had never missed that bus? In that case she would have had nothing to regret, and—nothing to remember.

As she reached the small entrance hall Madame Blanchard came from the back premises.

"Ah! Mam'selle," she greeted, "so you are ready to leave us."

"Yes, and I don't want to," Sanchia confessed. "I really have fallen in love with Saint Pierre."

"Then you will come back to us—next year perhaps?"

Sanchia shook her head. "I am afraid not. I have to work, Madame."

"But not always. One day you will have the honeymoon—do you not think Saint Pierre is the spot for your honeymoon?"

47

Sanchia laughed. "First I must find a bridegroom, you know."

"But certainly! What difficulty is that? Such a charming *jeune fille* surely had no scarcity to choose from." Madame stopped staring out through the open doorway as the car which had approached unnoticed swept into the Inn yard and was brought to a halt with a swift application of brakes. Almost at the same moment the driver was out of it and striding into the house.

"But see!" exclaimed Madame. "Here is Monsieur Adrian to bid Mam'selle adieu."

"That is the very last thing I want to do," Adrian announced. "Thank heaven I have caught you, Miss March! I'm depending on you to help me in a very difficult emergency."

# 5

## I

For a moment Sanchia stared at him, too surprised to take in clearly what he had said.

"Come in here." He turned towards a room leading off the hallway and thrusting open the door stood aside for her to enter. Then inviting Madame Blanchard to follow, with a gesture, he walked after them both and shut the door.

"What has happened?" asked the landlady anxiously. "There is something wrong at the Château?"

"There certainly is," he replied. "This morning my aunt fell down the steps outside her room and has hurt herself badly," and, when Madame Blanchard broke into a horrified spate of words, "Wait, please! Let me explain." He looked at Sanchia. "As I think I have mentioned, my aunt is already a victim of arthritis; she received treatment which has had miraculous effect, but she is not as strong as she likes to believe she is. Apart from the fact that she has now torn some muscles and suffered considerable bruising—at over seventy a fall is not a good thing. The doctor says she is badly shocked and she must lay up for some days. She ought, of course, to go into hospital, but she absolutely refuses to. Unfortunately the clinic, which our physician and friend runs, is full up; they are short staffed so that it is impossible to spare a nurse. This is where you come in,

Miss March. Can I rely on you to take the case? I understand from what you have told me that you are temporarily disengaged."

Sanchia knew there was no reason why she should not do what he plainly expected her to. Here was a ready-made job being thrust at her, plus the opportunity to stay in the place which such a little while ago she had so hated the idea of leaving. Yet she found herself hesitating, saying almost protestingly, "But, Mr. Carnforth, all my arrangements for returning to England are complete, and—"

"You will have to look for work when you get there, will you not?"

"Yes, but—"

"You are a nurse, are you not? And here is a sick woman much in need of your help—I thought nurses were trained to a sense of duty, of dedication? Perhaps I am wrong," he said, an undertone of biting sarcasm in his voice which had hardened in a way that matched the cold annoyance in his eyes. Suddenly Sanchia was again taken back to their first moment of acquaintance— the coldly formal man who had resented his interrupted drive was looking at her again with that same chilly hauteur. All at once she was sure that it would be quite possible to dislike him quite a lot. His 'charm' was plainly something he very easily shed!

"But, Mam'selle, you cannot refuse!" exclaimed Madame Blanchard. "Think! 'M'sieur Adrian came to your assistance when—"

"Be quiet, Adele! That has nothing whatever to do with this!" exclaimed Adrian.

But hadn't it? It seemed to Sanchia that Madame had managed to make her position ten times more difficult.

And Madame was a determined woman. In spite of Adrian's angry protest she insisted, "*Regardez, Mam'selle.* If you are concerned about your belongings at the hotel, Babette shall go now with Mario, and if you will give her your keys you can trust her to pack everything and bring it safely to you. Would not that be the way to arrange?"

"I had not thought of that," Sanchia admitted reluctantly. "It was because—" She bit her lip, beginning to be as angry with herself as she felt with the cold-eyed man who was watching her. After all, she *was* under an obligation to him, and this was an emergency. She had admitted to him yesterday that she would have to go 'wherever she was sent', and at least she knew something—though little enough, in all conscience—about these people. Beginning to be annoyed with herself now for what common sense and humanity told her was quite inexcusable behaviour, she looked towards Adrian again. Before she could speak he said curtly, "Please decide quickly. If you are unwilling to do as I ask, then I must see what can be done elsewhere."

"There is no need," she said quietly. "I will do all I can. Even if it is only a temporary arrangement."

"Good. Then, if you will write to the hotel, and give Babette your keys, she can see that your luggage is brought safely to you. Give the Château d'Aureoul as your address. The name is well known to the manager. Wait though," he added. "I will telephone him myself and explain. Meanwhile perhaps you will write that note and talk to Babette." With a brief nod he went quickly out of the room.

"Ah, but this is good," said Madame Blanchard, all smiles now. "I feel the great relief. I know that Madame la Comtesse will be looked after as she should be. If it was not that Babette is too young and has not the experience to take on my duties, I would have gone to Madame myself."

"Surely there must be people in the house who could look after her until a nurse was found?" asked Sanchia.

Madame pursed her lips. "There are servants, but is it

not plain that Madame must not be excited or upset? You have the authority of your profession. You can doubtless—manage Madame."

Sanchia was a little startled at the veiled suggestion that the old countess might not be easy to manage. However, she would soon find out whether her patient was ready to be co-operative or otherwise—and having taken the job she had every intention of seeing it through.

## II

There was notepaper and pen and ink on a desk in one corner of the room and without loss of time she sat down to write her instructions. She had given the note and her keys to Babette who, though she was trying to hide her excitement and was suitably concerned over what had happened, was delighted at the idea of taking Sanchia's place in the van with Mario. She was assuring Sanchia that she need not worry that any of her belongings would be left behind, when Adrian returned.

"That is all arranged," he announced, "there will be no trouble. And now, if you are ready, Nurse—"

"Quite ready," she agreed. She had settled her account and having bade Madame Blanchard au revoir followed him out to the waiting car.

Helping her in, he took his seat beside her, and drove off. But although both the professional and the humanitarian in her told his companion that it was her duty to do what she was called on to in this unexpected crisis she had not really shed her former reluctance. And how stupid that was! she thought. For did she not know perfectly well that if anyone had told her yesterday that she would be staying in this enchanting place for an indefinite period, she would have been sure that she was out of her mind to think of refusing such a chance. Yet how near she had been to doing so; though if her life had depended on being able to explain why, she could not have done it.

It could not be because of reluctance to get too involved in the affairs of Monsieur Adrian Carnforth. Or was it?—could it be because she had discovered that in spite of his great charm (which he could so evidently turn on when it pleased him to) it might be quite possible to violently dislike being—well, bossed about! He had certainly shown an arrogance which was unattractive, this morning. And then with a sudden revulsion she thought, I *am* being unfair! Of course he's worried over his aunt.

Anyway, as a nurse, it was up to her to respond to what Matron would describe a little pedantically as 'the call of duty'. She could not understand her reluctance to become an inmate of the Château d'Aureoul.

Yesterday she had wondered whether she was expected to speak first; today she was determined not to—and so for a time the drive proceeded in complete silence.

# 6

## I

"You feel I have bludgeoned you into this, don't you?"

Sanchia came out of her rather depressed reverie and looked round at the speaker. Watching the road ahead he added calmly, "No doubt you are right, but what else could I do?"

To her surprise she found herself agreeing. "Nothing, I suppose—since I was the nearest port in a storm."

"What an unreasonable sex yours is," he said. "Good heavens! You tell me you love your work, that you are not happy about the kind of patient you might get. You also tell me that you have fallen in love with your surroundings, but when a perfectly good chance of staying in them comes along you have to be practically blackmailed into taking it. Otherwise you would simply have handed it up. Is it because there is someone important who is expecting you back in England?"

"No, of course not," she replied.

"You are not engaged to be married—or anything like that?" he asked bluntly.

"I am not."

His lips twitched, and glancing briefly round he told her, "You would be entirely within your rights if you told me to mind my own darned business. I apologise. I merely asked because it would have been—awkward to find that you had an added reason for disliking me."

"Mr. Carnforth—please don't be absurd." But it was no use. She felt her resentment fading.

"Why don't you want to come?" he asked bluntly.

"I don't know," she answered. "Perhaps—well, this is a long way from my friends—and it *is* a foreign country. Anyhow, I hope I can be of help."

"I am sure you can," he told her. Then slowing the car down, "The truth is I disliked the idea of my aunt being in the hands of a stranger—"

"But *I* am stranger," she pointed out.

"Let me finish," he requested. "A stranger whom she might dislike, I don't think she will dislike you—though I confess frankly that you are likely to find her rather awkward at first. She resents feeling in any way helpless, and at times she is not easy to manage. She disliked the nurse she had last year and led her a dickens of a dance. Am I depressing you? Do you feel inclined to get out and walk back to Nice?"

She shook her head. "No. I'm used to difficult patients. I'll try not to give her cause to dislike me."

"I am pretty sure she won't—but she will take time to make up her mind. Handle her gently." His tone softened. "She's really a darling. When I was a kid she was the nearest thing I had to a mother. I used to spend most of my holidays here, and my cousin Blaise—who was the only son and heir, was like an elder brother. He was killed in the last war. That was his parents' tragedy."

"Oh! How sad!" Sanchia exclaimed. "And she had no other children?"

"None. As you are going to live in the Château I had better put you wise to things," he said, "or you may get muddled as to who is who! Incidently, Tante Hélène is my mother's sister— I may have told you this. On my Uncle the Comte's death the title finally died out. But the Château and all that goes with it is my aunt's. Remember—ill or well, she is the mistress of the house, and what she says goes. Don't at any time let anyone make you unhappy—or uncertain who to take directions from. Hello! here we are," he finished abruptly as they came in sight of a pair of wrought-iron gates behind which, set well back in its courtyard, the Château d'Aureoul stood.

Seeing the old house at close quarters Sanchia decided it was larger than it had appeared from a distance. It was marvellously picturesque; later she learnt that in the far-away days of Comte René of Provence, when the troubadours travelled the country singing the love songs they made, to beautiful ladies, it had been a setting for romance; but it had also been a fortress guarding the land surrounding it for many miles. It came to Sanchia when she looked at it now that this old house, reigning so peacefully over the lovely landscape, had known many, many adventures.

Well, here was a strange girl coming to discover what it held for her. If it held no adventures, she knew that at least it offered a challenge to her skill and her ability to adapt herself to what she had just been told were the vagaries of a patient who was not always easy to manage.

Oh well! She had been forced to come here, and if the experiment failed, Mr. Adrian Carnforth would have none but himself to blame!

There was a lemon tree with plump fruit showing among the dark leaves in the courtyard and on either side of the shallow steps leading up to the wide entrance doors slender cypresses stood like sentinels.

As the car stopped the doors were flung open and an elderly manservant came quickly down the steps and helped Sanchia to alight.

Following her Adrian asked, "Is Madame la Comtesse still sleeping, Jules?"

"No, Monsieur. She has been awake for half an hour and asking where you had gone. Celeste is with her."

Adrian turned to Sanchia. "I think we had better go straight up," he said. "Jules, Mademoiselle has come to nurse my aunt. See that a room is prepared for her."

"Will it not be better if I sleep for the present in Madame la Comtesse's room?" Sanchia asked. "She may need me in the night, if she is in pain."

He frowned thoughtfully. "That's true. Only I am afraid—but we will think about that later. You told Madame that I had gone to fetch a nurse, Jules?"

"*Oui, Monsieur.* She was not pleased."

Golly! thought Sanchia, it's begun already! But she was not really dismayed. Suddenly she realised that she was in harness again. Here was her first case without Sister to direct her—the only people to whom she would be responsible were the doctor, and the patient's relatives. She asked:

"Did Doctor—Driscoll, did you say . . . ?"

Adrian nodded. "He had to rush off, but he's coming along again this evening."

"Has he left any instructions?"

"He left a note. I believe she is to have another injection. He said you would know anything else that had to be done." Adrian gave her a humorous look. "I told him where you had trained. He seemed to think you were not likely to go wrong."

That was comforting at any rate, she thought, going up the steps beside him. But they certainly took it for granted that I would come!

She wished she could have arrived in the added authority of her uniform—or at least been able to wear something a little nearer resembling it, than the pink linen frock in which she had set out two days ago.

Thanks to Babette's ministrations the frock was as fresh-looking as when she had left Nice in it, but she felt it was a quite unsuitable garment in which to enter a sickroom where she was to take charge. However, that depended on how conventional-minded the patient was: pretty much that way she imagined.

They entered a wide hall from which rooms opened out on either side. Glass doors at the end of it showed a vista of lawn and a flower garden sloping away beneath a stone terrace. An exquisitely graceful staircase led upward to a sun-flooded landing above.

"Shall I lead the way?" Adrian asked.

"If you will, please." She was following him again then, too interested in her surroundings to feel nervous of what she was nevertheless sure was the ordeal before her. After all, this was not an ordinary case and she wondered how her evidently formidable patient would greet her.

Leaving the upper landing, they traversed a maze of corridors before reaching the short flight of steps which led to a door shutting off the countess's private apartments. Adrian paused at the bottom of the steps. "This is where she fell," he said. "I suppose that she must have caught her heel, the carpet had been left loose, though I cannot understand how that happened. Except that new carpet was laid yesterday, and the men must simply have left it unclipped. On the other hand my aunt examined it herself, and says she noticed nothing wrong —anyhow, some careless person is to blame. I haven't had time to go into the whys and wherefores of it yet."

The door was opened by a woman in a black dress and lace apron—very typically a lady's maid of the old kind. She was tight-lipped with greying hair, and in spite of the deferential way in which she addressed Adrian, it struck Sanchia that she was decidedly on the defensive; the kind who resented anyone trespassing on what she considered her business. She dropped a half-curtsey. "Monsieur Adrian, Madame la Comtesse has been asking for you," she informed.

"So I heard," he said. "Is she feeling any better?"

"*Non, Monsieur. La pauvre*! She is still in pain. I

told her you had gone to fetch a nurse, and she was—upset." She darted a look at Sanchia which changed abruptly from hostility to surprise. "Ah! but you did not manage to find the nurse!"

Without replying he put her aside, and following him Sanchia found herself entering a large exquisitely-furnished bedroom. But at this stage it was not the surroundings that interested her. Her eyes went instantly to the four-poster bed in which, beneath the silken covering, an unexpectedly small figure appeared almost lost among the pillows.

Her first impression of Madame la Comtesse d'Aureoul was of a pair of grey eyes which would have been startlingly like her nephew's, if what Sanchia guessed to be their usual keeness had not been filmed by the effects of the narcotic which was still making their owner drowsy, and a voice which in spite of its fretfulness still held an incisive note. But it hardly took a minute to realise that the face framed in short curling white hair still retained more than just traces of what in her youth must be striking good looks.

"So you are back. What is this about a nurse? I told you and that obstinate fool doctor, that I would not have a nurse; Celeste is quite capable of looking after me."

"No doubt," replied Adrian cheerfully. "Celeste will still be around, *chérie*, but here is Nurse March to do all the hard work."

A slight but decisive movement beneath the bedclothes advertised angry impatience, but though she glared at Sanchia the countess made no comment, and it was clear that she was still partially under the painkiller, though not sufficiently so to prevent her wincing at the effect of any movement.

"Let me help you, Madame la Comtesse," said Sanchia gently. "You look very uncomfortable." And in a moment

59

she had lifted the invalid into an easier position, rearranged her pillows, and settled her again. "There, isn't that better?"

She was rewarded by what could only be described as another glare, but it was accompanied by a grudging, "Thank you."

"Now, *chérie*, please do what the doctor, and Nurse, want you to," urged Adrian. "I am going to leave you now, and you must try to sleep as much as possible—isn't that so, Nurse?"

"Yes. And you will feel much better tomorrow," said Sanchia.

"How the devil can I sleep, when this confounded leg is torture?" the invalid demanded with surprising venom. "What fools you all are!"

Sanchia looked at Adrian, lowering her voice. "I think she should be due for another injection, but I don't know what the doctor's instructions are."

"He wrote this down." The maid produced a paper from the pocket of her apron, and was handing it to him when he ordered in a voice startlingly like his aunt's.

"Give it to Nurse. It is for her, is it not?"

"*Oui, M'sieur.* That is—"

"Then give it to her. You should have done so before."

"But it was not certain that there would be a nurse," Celeste pointed out. "I am sorry." But it was not with at all a good grace that she handed over the doctor's instructions.

Bending down again, Adrian murmured something in his aunt's ear, then with a smile and a nod to Sanchia moved towards the door, saying, "I will leave your patient to you now, Nurse. We will meet again later." A moment after the door shut silently behind him and Sanchia knew that the responsibility for all future developments in

Madame la Comtesse's blue and rose coloured bedchamber were hers.

Well, she had never been afraid of responsibility. But she could not help feeling that she had never met it under quite such daunting circumstances.

## II

But in spite of the drawbacks of knowing how unwelcome she was, and of Celeste's very evident jealous resentment, within a quarter of an hour Sanchia had everything going her way.

The bedroom was only one of the suite of four, both a bathroom and a large dressing room led off it and beyond that again was Madame's sitting room. It took only a very short time to find out that, in spite of her employer's conviction, Celeste would have made an inadequate nurse, her ideas of what should or should not be done in the way of running a sickroom being sketchy in the extreme. In the first place she had a fixed prejudice against fresh air; every window was tightly shut and almost all daylight screened out.

When Sanchia flung the windows wide and merely shaded the light from her patient's eyes the French woman protested that Madame was the victim of a *courant d'air* which would surely cause pneumonia. She agreed "The doctor had said the room must not be airless, but—"

Madame herself, having submitted to a second injection which the doctor had left ready, been given a cooling drink and adroitly lifted into a more comfortable position, murmured thanks and shut her eyes. Although no feat of imagination could have made Sanchia believe that her ministrations were received gratefully, they were at least submitted to.

While some young women in the nurse's place would have curtly dismissèd Madame's maid, Sanchia endured her continual presence, but she was grateful when going to answer a soft tap on the door, Celeste disappeared through it—evidently called elsewhere.

Left alone, Sanchia drew a chair near the bed and sat down. Now that she had leisure to study its sleeping occupant without having to encounter the cold displeasure of the expression that had greeted her, her impression of the old lady's good looks strengthend.

She was still beautiful, and must in her youth have been superb. But it could never have been mere empty beauty; there was a great deal of character in her face. Studying it, Sanchia was impressed by the old lady's likeness to Adrian, though it was not possible to pinpoint any particular sameness in feature—except in the brows which in the aunt had been tidied into perfect arches.

And Adrian could be just as ruthless as this formidable relative; she was sure of that when his eyes turned to grey agates and he looked as though your very existence was an insult! Ah! but how different was that warmer, friendlier side of him. *"But Monsieur Adrian is charming!"* Barbette's enthusiasm came echoing back to her and she laughed to herself. How right Babette was, and thank heaven that if her patient proved very difficult he would still be in the background.

But it did not occur to Sanchia how strongly he was in her thoughts, or how easy it might be to fall under the spell of that charm: to the detriment of one's peace of mind.

The patient slept on as her nurse had expected her to, and since Sanchia had no luggage to unpack and for the time being her duties were nil, she began to find time lying heavily on her hands as the morning moved towards noon. There were things that she wanted doing; Madame

La Comtesse's room was beautifully designed and luxurious, but the nurse in Sanchia had already decided that she would have liked certain alterations to be made. The four-poster bed, for instance, which stood in a deep recess, should be moved nearer the windows.

It was a lovely room. Looking round it, she saw every sign not only of luxury, but perfect taste.

The colour scheme was in delicate shades of blue and rose du Barry; the walls panelled in blue, and the hangings and upholstery of dusty rose. A blue Chinese carpet with a border of rose lay on the floor. There were white rugs beside the bed, and in front of the Louis Quinze dressing-table. On the gleaming surface of pale polished walnut lay a toilette set of silver-gilt, very simply designed, set with tiny pearls and turquoise enamel ornamenting the brushes, comb and hand mirror. Looking round her Sanchia thought that though to describe the dominating note as 'simplicity' might sound like an anachronism, it was entirely appropriate. This was undoubtedly the room of a wealthy woman, but there was nothing ostentatious or over luxurious about it. There was no wardrobe, but Sanchia's brief glimpse into the dressing room had shown a wall of sliding-doored cupboards with big mirrors and a day-bed.

She could easily have made herself better acquainted with the other rooms. But perhaps it was the certainty that that would be regarded as trespassing which kept her strictly within the bounds of the bed and bath rooms. And even there, she decided ruefully, her absence would have been more appreciated!

Going softly across to the windows she lifted up the shade from one of them and peering out found herself looking down into a blossom-filled garden which reminded her at once of some she had seen in England. There were masses of roses filling the beds and climbing and tumbling over arches and pergolas. Some of the beds were bordered with pale-coloured pinks, others with many-hued pansies or mauve cherry-pie. To find that this house possessed such an English garden suddenly made her feel more at home, and she wondered instinctively if Adrian had not something to do with that—Somehow it always came back to Adrian. After all, though he might have looked upon this place as his second home he was still an exile. She had not forgotten the shadow in his eyes and the bitter little twist to his mouth when he had said that the house in East Anglia was in other hands. *"Temporarily—I hope."* He must miss it. After all, the roots of those whose name he bore were rooted deeply in the soil. She remembered that beautiful old house well, and knew that if it had been hers she would have hated to know that strangers were living in it.

And yet—somehow he seemed part of this place too. An unconscious sigh escaped her as she dropped the blind and turned back towards the bed. Almost at the same moment the dressing room door opened noiselessly and Celeste beckoned to her. When Sanchia joined her the lady's maid said softly, "You are to sleep in here. It will be arranged for you."

"Oh, that will be good," Sanchia told her. "I shall be near if Madame should need anything in the night. Thank you, Celeste."

"It is not my arrangement," the woman said stiffly. "It is Monsieur Adrian's order. I don't think Madame will like it. But—" she shrugged.

The alternative would have been to sleep in the countess's bedroom, but Sanchia refrained from pointing that out, explaining instead that she was expecting her luggage to be brought from Nice later. Then remembering with a slight sense of shock the relationship between the countess's lady's maid and Babette she explained further, finishing with: "So Babette is very kindly collecting it for me."

"I would not say 'kindly'. She will be pleased enough to do it since it makes the excuse for a fête with that Mario," was the sour comment, and then, "But, Mamselle, Monsieur is expecting you down to lunch. At one o'clock."

"Oh—" Sanchia began, and stopped, feeling that at this stage she could not very well say she would rather have her meals alone somewhere, for though it should be easy enough to serve them in the now vacant boudoir there might be objections. She would have to talk to Adrian about that.

"In that case you will stay with Madame, will you not?" she asked. "She may sleep on for some time—"

"If she wakes I am capable of looking after her," was the instant, offended, response.

"I know you are," replied Sanchia determined to overcome the woman's resentment. "You will be a great help to me. You know all Madame la Comtesse's habits and tastes. How about her diet? It should be very light today and perhaps tomorrow, and then you will see that her meals are right, and served punctually." (Quite unnecessary, she was sure, but it seemed very wise, if there was not to be an atmosphere of perpetual antagonism, to induce Celeste to feel she had some authority.)

"You are very right," the maid agreed. "It will be necessary for someone to see that those lazy ones in the kitchen do their duty—that Thérèse! she thinks *she* knows Madame's taste. *She* will make the menu—Madame will not be bothered ever about the cuisine. It is left to Thérèse who will give Madame what she thinks. It was different when Blanchard was chef—" (So it is not only me she hates having anything to do with Madame! thought Sanchia.)

Celeste said a trifle more amicably, "It will be time for you to go down, Mam'selle. The apéritifs are served in the salon—Jules will show you where."

So having received her marching orders and tidied

herself, Sanchia proceeded to make her way downstairs.

But it was not as easy as she had hoped. Though she had thought she would remember her way back to the main landing, on leaving Madame's suite she became involved once again in that maze of passages which appeared to bring her in sight of the staircase.

She was hesitating which way to go next when from the dimness of the passage before her a tall white-clad figure emerged as silently and suddenly as if it had risen from the floor. With a gasp of astonishment she found herself looking up into a dark face lit by a pair of inscrutable eyes that were only just quite black in contrast to their owner's skin. Though she was usually able to adjust herself to the unexpected, she was so startled by this sudden, quite silent apparition that she could only stare. Then,

"*Pardon, Mam'selle*," the man said, raising his clasped hands in an upward gesture. "You are looking for someone?" His French was halting and he spoke with a strange accent.

Realising now that this was a human being, she recovered herself. "I was to go down to the salon," she explained. "Will you please direct me."

With another salaam, but without a word, he turned and led the way. Stalking ahead he seemed very tall in his white jacket and tight-fitting trousers, a turban twisted about his head. She could not help wondering how on earth he came to be here—somehow he seemed so incongrous in these surroundings—and was speculating on his nationality. Although she had come in contact with many different races at the hospital, somehow she could not place this copper-skinned, silent-footed man. But in a very short time she had followed her guide out on to the landing and saw the staircase ahead.

"Oh! thank you," she exclaimed. "I know my way now."

The man bowed and making another salute had turned and was swallowed in the shadows of the passage behind him so quickly that it almost seemed he must simply have vanished altogether.

A puzzled little crease between her brows, Sanchia descended to the hall and found Jules waiting for her.

"I lost my way," she explained. "I hope I am not late."

"No, no, Mademoiselle, there is plenty of time," he assured. Then ushering her across the hall he opened a door and as it closed behind her Adrian came quickly across the floor.

"Oh, there you are," he greeted. "Good morning. Is everything all right?"

"Good morning. Yes, everything is O.K. My patient is sleeping peacefully, Celeste is with her." She did not feel the inner conviction which matched the assurance with which she spoke had anything to do with the fact that 'Monsieur Adrian' was there again and the last thing she would have been inclined to do was realise the reason for that abrupt lifting of her spirits. She knew though that it was a distinct relief to find him alone; yesterday he had mentioned his cousin and that there was a guest in the house; she had expected to have to face strangers, and because she never found it easy to overcome shyness when meeting people socially—though she felt how stupid it was when she got on so easily with all those her work brought her in contact with—she had dreaded it.

Yet, in spite of everything, she had so quickly overcome the initial difficulties of getting to know Adrian Carnforth and was ready to own that the sight of him had power to banish all depression and that curious sense of apprehension which had descended on her just now.

"Good!" he approved. "Come and sit down and let me get you a drink." He pointed to a chair and turned back towards a table on which a tray of bottles and glasses stood.

"Nothing alcoholic, please," she begged.

He smiled round at her. "How very abstemious you are."

"I am on duty," she reminded him. "Anyhow, as I told you before, it makes me sleepy—even if I did not mind breathing it on my patient like Sairey Gamp!"

He gave her an approving glance. "Hello! You know your Dickens! Good girl. What shall it be. Orange juice? Tomato?"

"Orange, please." He really had the most charming smile and he was—terribly nice. The thought was involuntary, any prejudice entirely forgotten.

Bringing her glass across he said, "Don't let yourself be depressed if Tante Hélène is a bit prickly at first. As I told you, she loathes being helpless, poor dear. This is really most unfortunate."

"I wonder what really went wrong," Sanchia said. "Those are very shallow steps."

"And she is so completely used to them. The new carpet was laid yesterday and the man who did it must be to blame. Anyhow, the damage is done, and she will be laid up—or anyhow unable to get around, for some considerable time, I suppose. And falls are not good for old ladies—though it always seems *lèse-majesté* to refer to Tante Hélène as old."

"I am afraid that kind of injury takes six weeks at least to mend," said Sanchia. "But of course she would not be in bed all that time—in fact she won't have to be— but when I have seen Dr. Driscoll I shall know what he proposes."

"You will stick it out, won't you?" he asked.

"Oh yes—unless she sends me packing." If she was surprised at the sudden firmness of her decision she hardly realised it. But since she had let herself be 'dragooned' into taking the case and he was so concerned about his aunt, it seemed difficult to let him down. After all, she decided, Madame Blanchard was right. He did come to my rescue.

"What are you looking so serious about?" Adrian asked. "Is the thought of having to remain here so depressing? Saint Pierre is only a comparative stone's-throw away, and you are ready to end the love affair almost before it began."

"It had not really started, you know," she reminded him. "Perhaps I don't want to get deeply involved."

"Just a flirtation? Too bad for Saint Pierre."

"But surely saints are above such things?"

He laughed. "Anyway I suppose it would be unjust to expect you not to exercise your delightful sex's age-old privilege of changing your mind." Though he spoke lightly she detected a faint note of bitterness behind the words. There was no time to wonder if she was mistaken, for at that moment voices on the terrace outside the long open windows drew his attention in that direction.

"Are we late, Adrian? Mr. Vernon's car developed an allergy to hills, and we had to push her up the last one."

The speaker paused, framed in the open window, and looking towards her, Sanchia thought involuntarily: Gosh! what a beauty!

"Now that's not quite fair, Mrs. Danvers," protested the man who had followed the new arrival into the room. "It sure wasn't bad manners, or a leaning to delinquency that made her stall. It was just an empty tank."

"Of course it was—" The girl broke off staring at Sanchia. "I didn't know you had a guest, A."

Meeting the speaker's hard stare as Adrian introduced her, Sanchia's second impression was that undoubtedly decorative as this young woman was, she was as hard as the proverbial nails; spoiled, and decidedly allergic

69

to her own sex. At the same time she was conscious of a curious feeling of revulsion which had nothing to do with those impressions, and which she was to remember in the future.

"But how kind of you." Laure Danvers' voice somehow matched the coldness of her violet eyes. "But why didn't you get a trained nurse, A?"

"Miss March is a fully trained nurse," he informed.

The beauty turned her head to stare at Sanchia again. "I see. But my dear cousin, I *am* disappointed. I really thought you had got yourself a glamorous girlfriend—not that professionalism detracts from glamour," she added laughingly. "I am sure that quite a profusion of trained nurses match their television images. But I *am* disappointed in you, Adrian."

"Sorry about that." He spoke coolly, but it was obvious that Mrs. Danvers' bad taste annoyed him, while Sanchia felt her cheeks suddenly burning.

"Oh well, I really must get rid of the dust," Laure said lightly. "And I'm sure Mr. Vernon would like to wash. Just one little quick one, please, then we'll be off."

"Meanwhile it might be an idea to introduce Mr. Vernon," observed Adrian, angry at the omission which Laure's questionable taste had caused. "Miss March, this is Mr. King Vernon who has done us the honour to come all this way to taste our wines."

The tall American shook hands. "Which is something I shall never regret. For apart from that I have been very happy to meet delightful new friends," he said. "This visit will be a treasured memory." His glance in Laure's direction was brief, but it was plain to Sanchia that this nice, good-looking Bostonian had fallen a victim to the lovely lady's charms.

Then, having drunk the Martinis which Adrian mixed for them, the other two departed to tidy themselves.

Looking after Mrs. Danvers, Sanchia decided with

unusual emphasis that she was grateful that this fair lady was not her employer. Naturally tolerant, she had learnt enough about the various types of human nature with which she had come in contact to make excuses for their foibles; also, beauty of any kind had always filled her with warm delight. But she could not remember ever before taking an instant dislike to anyone, or knowing so plainly that they had done just that to her. *I hope to goodness I shan't have much to do with her!* she thought ruefully.

"Will you have another of those, or are you in need of something stronger?"

She looked round and found Adrian watching her.

"No more, thanks."

"I am sure that you must be starving," he said. "I am afraid we shall have to wait for Vernon; but, knowing my cousin, I refuse to eat a ruined luncheon. So we will not wait for her."

Sanchia laughed. "Don't worry about me, I shall survive. I don't suppose Mrs. Danvers will be all that long."

"Inexperience makes you an optimist," said Adrian drily. "Time is a mode of thought with my coz, maybe because she was born in the East and lived there for so many years."

"Oh! I suppose that accounts for—" Sanchia began impulsively, and broke off.

"Yes?" he prompted.

"Well, I nearly lost myself on the way downstairs, and an Eastern manservant—at least I suppose he was an employee—directed me."

"Yes, that was Mohamed. He's always somewhere around; he is Laure's special henchman and almost her shadow," Adrian explained. "I can't stand the fellow myself, but my aunt endures him. You see, he's been with Laure since she was a very small mite; when she was born her father had a post in Egypt, then he moved to Singapore and Mohamed went back with him. He—Mohamed—married a Chinese woman who was Laure's amah*; she is dead now, but Mohamed has managed to hang on." Sanchia noticed that though he had spoken lightly, his face set, and she decided that he had very little liking for any of the Danvers set-up.

Suddenly remembering what she had wanted to discuss with him, she said, "Mr. Carnforth, I really must do something about a uniform. If I sent to England it would take ages to reach me. Do you think there is somewhere in Nice where I could get what I need?"

"Ask the doctor," he told her. "I think you will find he will help, if you think it is as necessary as all that."

"I do," she assured him firmly.

"Well, don't worry. Ask Dr. Driscoll."

"Thank you," she said gratefully.

King Vernon came back just then, and whether Adrian's determination that the meal should not be kept waiting had anything to do with it or not, when five minutes later lunch was announced, Laure met them at the dining room door.

It was apparent that she could hurry if it suited her. She had made a complete change of costume, substituting the white linen ensemble with a pale green shantung frock in the same expensively simple style.

When they sat down to lunch Sanchia immediately noticed Mohamed's presence. He appeared with exactly the same unexpectedness and having assisted Jules in serving the food glided about as silent-footed as a ghost, before taking his stand behind Laure Danvers' chair, where he remained, ready to anticipate her smallest need.

They had just begun the meal when the room door opened and a slightly drawling masculine voice asked,

* Nanny.

72

"Is there anything for a starving man? I've driven all the way from Monte in two hours without killing anyone, and I think I deserve to be fed."

Sanchia who was seated opposite Laure saw her expression change quickly from surprise to displeasure.

"Max! I thought you were not coming back until Saturday."

"But here I undoubtedly am, darling—your most devoted spouse. And how is my lady wife? No need to ask, with the evidence before me." Going round the table the new arrival dropped a light kiss on the cheek which Laure turned towards him, her face almost as expressionless as a mask.

"What are you doing here?" she asked.

"I give you one guess," he said carelessly. "But what is this I hear about our dear despot? What has she been doing to herself?"

"She had a fall," Adrian informed briefly.

"Did she indeed! How very careless of la tante. No really serious consequences, I trust?" said Danvers sauntering towards the place which Mohamed had prepared for him with almost magical speed.

"Nothing worse than an injured knee," replied Laure. "Nurse can tell you more about that if you are yearning for clinical details. But what am I thinking of!" she added quickly." Please forgive me, Mr. Vernon. You will have gathered this is my husband. Max, this is King Vernon from Boston. And Miss March—I suppose it should be Nurse March!—my husband."

Max had acknowledged the American with a rather cool nod, and a brief "How do you do." Then as his sleepy eyes turned to Sanchia they lost their languor. "Nurse? I don't believe it," he exclaimed." "Where's the starch?"

Immediately Sanchia knew that here was the type of man she detested, the type who was instantly aware of

73

any even reasonably attractive member of the opposite sex and determined to make them aware of him.

Adrian said coldly, "Miss March has very kindly broken her holiday to undertake the care of Tante Hélène."

"If la tante allows her to," observed Laure with a brittle little laugh.

"I say! Is it really as bad as that—I mean is she going to be a—to have to lay up for long?" This time the question was directly to Sanchia. To her grateful relief just then his attention was diverted to the plate which had been put before him, and he was obliged to remove his too intent gaze from her face.

It would have been difficult to find a more perfectly matched pair, as far as looks were concerned, than Laure Danvers and her husband—Max was black-haired and dark-eyed, not as tall as Adrian and with just a suggestion that it would be easy for him to run too much to flesh as middle age approached, and his dark good looks made a perfect foil for the blonde beauty of his wife. But, while Sanchia acknowledged his good looks, it had not taken her long to make up her mind on two points— that she did not like the type, and that in spite of the almost elaborate affection of his greeting, there was no real love between those two. Several times during what she remembered always as the most uncomfortable meal she had ever sat through, she caught him watching his wife, a sardonic smile on his lips.

After answering him briefly once or twice Laure continued to concentrate her attention on the house guest. Always sensitive to atmosphere, Sanchia soon felt that there was a sense of strain between the three members of the household. As the meal progressed while Laure continued to entertain the American, whose admiration for her was almost too obvious, Max, turning his shoulder on Adrian, proceeded to find out all he could about the Comtesse's new nurse.

"I take it that you are one of Dr. Driscoll's young ladies," he said, those heavy-lidded eyes searching her face with an undisguised pleasure which brought the colour to her cheeks. "In that case you know this part of the world well."

She shook her head. "No. I have not yet met Dr. Driscoll."

Coming to her rescue Adrian said curtly, "The doctor could not spare one of his nurses. Miss March very kindly consented to help us out."

"How—lucky," murmured Danvers, and then ignoring Adrian he continued insistently to address his conversation to Sanchia. He asked if she knew Monte Carlo, and when the brief answer was that she had been there, enlarged on the fact that he himself had become utterly bored with the atmosphere of the Principality, though he expected that with the usual triumph of hope over experience it would lure him back in time.

"Which means that you did not have luck at the tables, Max," said Adrian bluntly.

Max shrugged the statement away, and Sanchia saw his wife dart a venomous look at him, though she made no comment.

"I was born without your luck, my dear Adrian," Max said. "Or shall I say with more sense of adventure? After, all, life is dull enough, heaven knows, without one becoming a turnip."

"There are different kinds of 'adventure'," observed Adrian with a return to his usual cool manner.

"How true. You have your—or rather la tante's—vines, etcetera, which make another kind of gamble."

"In which nature takes a hand—"

"Ah, but surely not only nature. There is always the unpredictability—shall we say?—of Madame la Comtesse," laughed Max.

What lay behind that seemingly innocent remark was

at present far from Sanchia's understanding, but seeing Adrian's lips set and the way that for a moment the two men regarded each other, she became more sure that they disliked each other intensely.

It was Danvers whose eyes first wavered, then turned again in her direction. But though as lunch progressed he tried to find out more about how she had come to be here, she was suddenly determined that he should not and skilfully parried his attempts.

She had never been more relieved than when the meal came to an end. But Max had not finished yet, and as they rose from the table he said in his lazy way, "Anyhow, I'm sure you will agree, Adrian, that our new nurse is a marvellous improvement on the last one. That starched, uniformed young woman really intimidated me last year, Miss March."

"Did she? Perhaps I shall, when I get into uniform," she said.

"Heavens above! Is that a warning?" he cried. "Honestly I suffer from an allergy to any reminder of illness. Don't I, Laure?"

His wife, on her way out of the room, looked round at him. "Do you? The only thing I noticed was that Nurse Macleod seemed to develop a decided allergy to you, darling. Don't make a nuisance of yourself," she added lightly. "Coffee in the salon, Miss March."

She went out of the room, and turning quickly to Adrian, Sanchia said, "Forgive me, I must go back to my patient," and without waiting for a reply, or glancing at Max, she hurried away. It might be an abrupt exit, but she felt that in another moment she would retort to Max Danvers' impertinent bad taste by being really rude —which might make things difficult, because after all he was Madame la Comtesse's relation, if only by marriage. It was not so difficult to find her way back as it had been to get her bearings earlier. This time she met no one, and entering Madame la Comtesse's bedroom again actually felt relief.

As she had expected, the comtesse was still sleeping, and having sent Celeste to get her own meal, and see that when Madame woke, a tray should be ready for her, she went through to the dressing room.

She found that it had already been arranged as charming and comfortable sleeping accommodation. A bed was made up, and a table arranged with a triple mirror, for her toilet things. But remembering Celeste's *"I do not know what Madame will say"* she felt a little worried, though as she must be within call if her patient should need her, this was the best way.

Anyhow, here she was—committed now to see this case through. Had it been foolish to fall in so easily with Adrian's plans? Then, remembering that hour in the dining room, she thought ruefully that it was no wonder that the odd intuition which often warned her away from unwise conduct had made her hesitate about agreeing to come here.

She might succeed in winning over her patient, but she was already certain that Adrian's cousin had taken a dislike to her and would do all she could to make her stay uncomfortable. Then with a characteristic flash of independence she decided: Well, that's just too bad! But whether she likes it or not this is my job now, and I mean to do it.

# 7

## I

Sanchia fastened her belt, and standing a little back
regarded her reflection in one of the long mirrors with
satisfaction which had nothing to do with the picture the
looking glass framed.

Though she had every right to be pleased with that
picture, it was doubtful if there ever was a girl less
conscious of her looks. Her pleasure came solely from the
fact that she was in uniform again. Nurse Sanchia March,
with the professional authority which she felt she really
needed.

Bless the doctor! she thought gratefully. He had been
so helpful. When, after her session with the man who,
in spite of what she understood were his many other
commitments, was the d'Aureoul family physician, she
had explained that she found herself stranded with
nothing but 'civvies' to wear, he had assured her that
need be the least of her worries; there would be no
difficulty in finding what she needed. At the clinic which
he ran, the nurses' uniforms were found for them, and
if she would write down her 'vital statistics' he would
see that she was sent what she needed.

She hardly dared hope, though, that the other problems which littered her paths could be so easily solved.

But she was to find that things were easier than she
had expected them to be that morning. Rather to her

dismay when she entered her patient's bedroom she found her already awake.

The Comtesse's greeting was coolly non-committal, but, having requested that Celeste should be rung for, the invalid submitted to her nurse's ministrations with surprisingly good grace, though the way those shrewd grey eyes watched her—so obviously taking in every detail of her appearance—was more than a little embarrassing.

But if Madame la Comtesse meant to make her nurse uncomfortable that young woman showed no outward sign of perturbation and when she had finished all that needed doing, she calmly left Celeste to take over. The maid had brought up Madame's morning tray of chocolate and brioche.

Sanchia allowed about twenty minutes to elapse before she returned to the room to find the patient alert and looking extremely ornamental, but deceptively frail. Having already had more than a hint of the old lady's toughness Sanchia could hardly repress a smile, though she frankly admired the fastidious daintiness of the picture her patient presented. Madame wore a powder-blue satin bedjacket over the shell-pink silk nightdress which she had earlier directed Sanchia to change her into. She was reading one of the morning papers which had been brought up to her, and looked up rather sharply. For a moment Sanchia sustained a probing stare. Then Madame raised her brows in a way that accentuated her likeness to her nephew.

"Ah!" she said. It was a curiously non-comittal sound and might have meant almost anything.

Sanchia said quietly, "You are looking much better, Madame."

"I am better. Just because I tumbled down does not mean that I am ill. I would like to get up. I can at least

79

sit in a chair, I presume—even if I have to hobble round like some decrepit wreck of ninety."

It was fortunate that Sanchia could understand the idiomatic French in which the other spoke; she had a strong idea that she was not expected to. If Madame was able to complain that her nurse could not understand her, it would be a good excuse for getting rid of her.

But since she did understand, she replied smilingly, "You do not need to be anything like ninety for an injury like yours to make you lame, Madame la Comtesse. But it will get better, you know. In a few days we will begin a new treatment, which will soon mend those muscles up."

The reply to that was merely an unbelieving little grunt. There was a pause, and then, "You speak very good French. Where did you learn it?"

"From my mother's mother, Madame. She was born in Provence."

A flicker of interest passed across the other's face. "Is that so?" Then, seeming to lose interest, she picked up the paper again. But when Sanchia began to move softly about the room, arranging things more as she wanted them, those keen eyes watched and Madame's thoughts were busy. Yesterday, apart from resenting the girl's presence, she had not been able to get more than a vague impression of her nurse's appearance. But she was conscious now of a distinct personality, and she admitted grudgingly to herself that the young woman was reposeful. Certainly she was not easily rattled! Now that her keen mind was working normally she had a very shrewd idea that Nurse March had not been an unknown quantity to her nephew; unless she—Madame—was very mistaken. But she was pretty sure that Celeste would know all about that.

Meanwhile, she was summing up her nurse with characteristic clarity.

Pretty? No, that was not the right word; too much

character in the downbent profile presented towards her for mere prettiness.

One of the comtesse's idiosyncrasies was her liking to herself arrange the flowers with which her rooms were freshly filled each morning. If someone else had to take over that task she invariably found something wrong.

Watching Sanchia's long fingers going deftly about her task, the crease between the old lady's brows disappeared.

"You like flowers?"

Sanchia, whose thoughts had been elsewhere, came back to her surroundings with a start and looked round to meet once again a somewhat daunting stare from her patient's grey eyes. (How like Adrian's those eyes were!) It had been Madame's nephew who had been occupying the thoughts of Madame's nurse, which was partly the reason for the suddenly added colour in her cheeks. Not that it occurred to her to feel in any way guilty; what, after all, could have been more natural than to remember the tangled circumstances of their acquaintance, and the mixture of charm and arrogance that made one wonder about him.

"Yes, Madame la Comtesse," she agreed quietly. "I love them."

"Ah! You have a way with them," was the unexpected announcement. "Have you learnt flower arrangement?"

"Oh no." Sanchia could not help laughing, thinking how little time she had ever had for such a hobby. "But I used to arrange a good many in hospital—when the patients were sent them," she explained, and then hesitatingly, "I hope you don't mind me arranging these, but—I thought they needed something doing to them. They looked so formal."

Madame said, "All the servants here are villagers—even Celeste. Excellent people who give wonderful service, but not exactly artistic, naturally." She added bluntly,

"I find the English just push flowers into vases."

"Oh, not all of them!" Sanchia protested.

Before the other could reply there came a light tap on the door. While Sanchia moved towards it, it opened and Mme. Danvers entered.

"Good morning, *chérie*, may I come in?" she asked.

"You seem to be already in. Good morning, Laure. Shut the door, please," said Madame coolly.

"Oh! I'm sorry." The newcomer turned back and having closed the door, moved swiftly across and bending down kissed her aunt first on one and then on the other cheek.

"Dearest," she cooed, "you're looking marvellous— though you cannot possibly be feeling it. I have been so worried about you all night."

Having finished her rearrangement of the roses, Sanchia, glancing in the direction of the bed saw the expression with which the old lady was regarding her niece reflected her sardonic tone.

Laure, apparently quite unaware of the cool response, drew a chair to the bedside and seated herself, obviously prepared for a cosy chat.

She certainly was a lovely thing, but though Sanchia still felt admiration for the picture the other girl made, she could not help noticing how studied every graceful movement was. All the time young Mme. Danvers was fully aware of her lovely self and the effect it was having on others. Up to now she had completely ignored the fact that there was a third person in the room, and Sanchia could not help knowing that here again Laure was out for effect. She was determined to make the nurse—who was paid for being here—realise the difference in their positions. And there was that hard mouth contradicting her exotic looks.

Her sense of humour coming to the surface, Sanchia turned away, though there was more than just a touch of distaste mingled with the amusement.

"But, Tante Hélène," Laure urged, "are you sure you are well enough to sit up? You must be terribly shaken."

"I am perfectly well, except for this confounded knee," the comtesse retorted with her old asperity. "Don't fuss, Laure! It bores me. I am not made of glass and a tumble has not broken me. In any case I am being very well looked after," she glanced towards Sanchia. "You and Nurse have met, have you not?"

"Yes. At lunch yesterday." Forced to the admission Laure gave the other girl a cool nod. "Good morning, Nurse, you need not wait. I will stay with my aunt—for as long as she can bear me," she added.

Ignoring this broad hint Sanchia addressed her patient. "Is there anything more you need just now, Madame la Comtesse? Or would you like me to leave you for a little while?" She consulted her wristwatch. "I'm due to give you your injection in twenty minutes."

"Then for twenty minutes I suggest you go and walk in the garden, my child. If you see Adrian you will please tell him when you think I shall be ready for him to come up." The tone in which Madame spoke and her smile were unexpectedly gracious.

Sanchia smiled back. "Thank you, Madame. Yes, I will tell Monsieur Adrian—or leave a message for him." Then with a slight inclination of her head in the directtion of the visitor she went out of the room.

Having shut the door closely behind her she indulged in a silent little laugh, but there was a crease between her brows while she made her way downstairs a few moments later. Laure certainly was a so-and-so! But she was sure the comtesse was not taken in by her nieces 'gush'; and not quite sure that Madame's graciousness towards herself had not been partly meant to annoy Mrs. Danvers. But why should Laure object to her being here?

she wondered. Because she's just naturally allergic to her own sex?

Whatever the reason it was plain enough the other had taken a dislike to her, and would probably do all she could to make things—uncomfortable. Oh, well, Nurse March decided, shrugging the idea away, no doubt I shall survive!

## II

Inside the room Laure murmured, "I am sure that young woman will do her utmost to keep you in order, *ma chére*."

"No doubt. She is very capable," the older woman agreed calmly.

Laure lowered her eyes, a flash of annoyance in them. It was unlike her aunt to be so amenable, and this cool acceptance of her—Laure's—suggestion was disturbing. The trouble was, Madame was quite unpredictable, and if she had really taken a fancy to her nurse that could be—anyway in her niece's opinion—very tiresome. Then looking up again she laughed lightly.

"Darling, she has yet to learn how very capable you are of cutting a bossy young woman down to size."

"No doubt, if the occasion arose," agreed Madame. "Up to the present I find her a pleasant antidote to that affliction who nursed me last year."

"Well darling, I hope she will be a success." Laure appeared to hesitate. Then, "But do you know who she is?" she asked.

"What do you mean?"

"My dear, I don't suppose you have guessed—how could you—that this is none other than the young woman who stopped Adrian on the road and made him late for dinner on Thursday? Remember?"

"Yes, I remember," said Madame.

"What an odd person he is," observed Laure. "He didn't tell us that he had parked her at the Veau d'Argent—where apparently he lunched with her the next day. Isn't he a dark horse?"

"How?" asked Madame.

"Well—don't you think he could have told us that she was still hanging around. When I first saw her I thought he had found himself a girl friend."

"I really don't see why, Laure. As for hanging around, I understood she was waiting until Mario could give her a lift back to Nice. It was lucky that Adrian caught her in time to persuade her to come here—as I understand there would have been considerable delay in getting another nurse. What is the matter?"

Laure had been unable to hide her surprised dismay at the discovery that the information which she had been sure would annoy her aunt was already in the old lady's possession.

"You—knew?" she asked.

"I guessed, and I do not see what all this is about."

"I—just thought you ought to be told." It would have been better to have left it there—or not to have interfered, but there was a stupid streak in the lovely Mrs. Danvers which had tripped her up more than once. She had obtained her own information from Babette, who was still thrilled at the 'romantic' circumstances under which Adrian and Sanchia had met. Laure had forgotten that Babette would also have told her aunt, Madame la Comtesse's maid. Smiling sweetly she said, "Well, darling, as long as you are happy that's all that matters."

"Certainly," Madame agreed coolly. "I really feel that Adrian's little adventure was to my advantage." Then with an abrupt change of subject, "So Max is back."

"Oh yes!" Laure exclaimed. "I was going to tell you" —but you always know everything as long as Celeste is there to keep you wise! she thought angrily. She was also sure that her aunt guessed the reason for Max's un-expected return without needing anyone to explain it.

"The joys of Monte Carlo have faded more quickly this time," Madame observed drily, but to her niece's relief she did not go further into the subject, asking instead about the guest who was leaving them today.

"He sent you all kinds of messages of thanks and commiseration," Laure told her. "He has gone for a last look at the vineyards with Adrian. Max sent his love too, he wants to know when he may come to see you."

"When I feel more inclined for visitors," was the reply.

"But surely Max is not a *visitor*?" Laure sounded reproachful. "He was shattered when he heard what had happened to you."

"Nice of him, but assure him that I shall survive. And now, my dear, you must run away. I want to rest before Nurse returns and has to pull me about."

Receiving such an uncompromising dismissal Laure rose. "All right, darling," she said. "If I am boring you—"

"I slept badly and I want to rest."

"Poor sweet! I know you hate it. But don't let that bit of starched efficiency bully you," advised Laure. "I really think you would have been better with a French girl—they are more *sympathique*—of course if we could have had a nursing sister from the convent that would have been ideal. Although," she gave a brittle little laugh, "perhaps a devoted nun would not have been so popular with Adrian—and Max certainly turned an appreciative eye on the young woman."

"Max," said the comtesse with sudden tartness, "always turns an appreciative eye on anything decorative in petticoats."

Max's wife laughed again, "Oh! I'm used to that—there's no harm in it—really—"

86

"Hum!"

There was a slight pause, while Laure examined her beautifully-kept hands. Then: "I suppose she *is* decorative," she said, sounding more grudging than she realised. "If you admire the type. Maybe I'm—ungenerous, but I always wonder what is going on behind that calm sort of mask that is a stock in trade of most nurses. Your last one was the bustling type, but no one could have accused her of being sexy."

"They could not, and I certainly would not use that modern vulgarism in connection with my present nurse. I am grateful that she is so decorative; plain young women depress me. Now, *ma chére*, run away and do not worry about me."

But when her niece had gone she lay staring thoughtfully into space, a crease between the brows that were so like Adrian's. There was something at the back of her mind that she was reluctant to examine, and it was a relief to even suspect that there might be a new problem to consider.

*I thought Adrian had found himself a girl friend.*

Well, why not? And why should Laure dislike the idea?

## III

In the weeks that followed, although Sanchia discovered that even in the peace and beauty of this heavenly spot some imperfections existed, blessedly the snags did not include her relationship with her patient. Very soon any trace of antagonism in Madame la Comtesse's manner had faded. If she was not always an ideal patient she was a surprisingly co-operative one—which had paid off where both patient and nurse were concerned.

Though the comtesse was as yet unable to do more than hobble round with the help of a stick, and though she was disinclined to accept her infirmity with anything like patience or fortitude, her irritation was never for her nurse. Sanchia had in fact grown extremely fond of the old lady and she felt sure that they would have been far more comfortable if Mrs. Danvers had decided at least to accept her presence as a necessary evil. But it was impossible not to know that the other girl both disliked her and resented her presence at the château.

However, Laure's was not the only bitchiness Sanchia had met with over the years; she could ignore it or at any rate take it in her stride. She was able to avoid Laure but her real headache was Max Danvers who never missed an opportunity of trying to turn their acquaintance into something more personal. Unfortunately it was not always possible to avoid his flirtatiousness and somehow whenever he managed to corner her, either his wife or Adrian was bound to appear on the scene.

Sanchia had been walking in her favourite part of the gardens—a secluded enough spot for her to hope to escape company, one morning, when the handsome Max had followed and was pacing beside her when they came face to face with Adrian.

Max's gay "Hello Adrian, since no one has told you three is not company, stay and add your persuasions to mine—I tell Nurse that she does not get half enough time to herself."

"And I tell Mr. Danvers that I get more than enough. Anyhow, I must go back now," Sanchia said, and aware that in spite of the cool bleakness of Adrian's eyes, her cheeks were burning, she made her escape. Almost at once she regretted her haste, and looking back she was regretting it now. It was the third time that Adrian had found her tête-à-tête with Max Danvers and she felt it would be understandable if he was beginning to believe that she was partly to blame—that in fact she must be encouraging the other man.

During her first week at the château she had seen

quite a lot of Adrian; he came each morning to visit the comtesse who usually told her. "Don't run away, Nurse." So she would go on arranging flowers, or whatever else she was doing and find Adrian drawing her into the conversation.

It had seemed that their relations were to continue along the lines which had begun on the day he had given her lunch and driven her out afterwards. How little she had dreamed then that there would be any chance of that acquaintance developing. Was it stupid to —mind because in the second week his former warmth had suddenly become more formal?

*Very stupid—more than stupid!* she told herself. First because he and his aunt were now back to discussing a certain amount of estate business again—after all, he was her manager, and he must have a lot of things on his mind, with the big estate plus the wine business to look after. Perhaps it was just her imagination that his manner towards her had changed—and anyhow what did it really matter?

Madame would not need her services for many more weeks, and this enchanted interlude would lie behind her, receding gradually into the past, until it was almost forgotten.

But she knew that last was not true. She might be forced to go away, but she would leave part of her heart behind her—with Saint Pierre; of course with Saint Pierre. Thinking of all this while she walked by the river that ran through the village, she sighed while she watched the river flowing below her, she was jerked from her reverie by a little crowd of children who were racing each other over the bridge and were close to her before she realised their presence.

One small girl lagged behind, holding a younger brother by the hand, while the latter, a sturdy three-year-old, tried to pull himself free.

"*Non, non, bébé,*" his sister protested. "Maman said *no*. You must not."

The children belonged to one of Madame Blanchard's helpers at the inn and recognising them Sanchia called a gay good day and asked, "What does he want, Marthe?"

"To put his feet in the water, Mam'selle. That silly Paul Roche let him yesterday—but Paul is a big boy and can hold him."

"Even if Paul can, your little brother should not be encouraged to go close to the river," protested Sanchia who had memories of things that had happened to more than one child allowed to play on the banks of a canal which ran near to her London hospital. "Take him home, Marthe."

"I'm going to, Mam'selle." Dragging her small brother along Marthe continued on her way.

Sanchia looked after them frowning. Marthe, not more than eight herself, was a slender child and the boy was a healthy little handful of wilfulness. She wondered if she should see them safely home, though the cottage where they lived was only a little way round the next corner and no doubt the mother would be looking out for them. Already a bend in the road had hidden them and Sanchia had resumed her walk when a scream rang out, echoed by another.

In an instant she was running in the direction of the sound. Another moment and she saw what had happened. Why, oh why did I not go with the children! she thought. Marthe, standing on the river bank was being held back by her mother while her small brother was nowhere to be seen. It was only a moment before Sanchia saw the boy struggling to get out of the water into which he had fallen.

"Wait," she called, thankful for her fluent French, and that she had picked up sufficient of the local patois to make herself understood. "I'll get him."

But the bank was steep there, and quickly as she

negotiated it the undercurrent had borne the child into deeper water before she could help. Without giving a thought to what she was doing she waded forward, reached for the small floating body, missed it and thrust forward again, realising to her horror that the child had gone under. Then as he appeared again she caught him by his jersey and using all her strength lifted and flung him to the bank from where his mother dragged him to safety.

Then for the second time Sanchia realised how strong the current was, and that she was hampered by the dragging weight of her wet skirt. She clutched desperately at a branch of the overhanging willow and was clinging to it when a man's voice shouted, "Hold on—" then "Damn it, you've got to swim!" But suddenly she did not seem to have the strength to fight that sinister undercurrent and it was not until she found herself on the bank half pushed, half dragged upward that she knew she had lost moments of her life which memory would never recapture.

She lay staring up at the sky and wondering vaguely how the water had turned blue. Then a pair of angry grey eyes were looking into hers and a furious voice demanding, "What the hell were you playing at—?"

If she made a reply it was drowned by other voices all exclaiming together. A sobbing woman kneeling beside her blessing her as the saviour of her child "sent by Our Lady of Pity and her Blessed Son" brought Sanchia struggling to her feet, half conscious of a supporting arm.

"But I did nothing," she protested. "Anyone would—"

"Never mind that now. Take Mam'selle and give her dry clothes before I drive her home," Adrian commanded. "Thank God I was passing. Hurry woman!"

Still just a little dazed, ten minutes later she was beside Adrian in his car, telling him, "But you are soaking."

"I won't hurt," he assured impatiently. "When you feel better you can tell me how all that happened. Good heavens, don't you know how dangerous the current is just there?"

She explained, adding rather vaguely: 'I suppose Marthe let go of the boy's hand and—he fell in."

"Little devil! He's the only son—they lost their other one, and he's thoroughly spoiled," said Adrian angrily, and then again: "Thank God I came along!"

"Thank God you did," she echoed. "I got cramp. Thank you—you certainly saved me—I shall be fine now."

"I'm sure you will—fine!" But though he sounded almost savagely sarcastic, as he took his eyes briefly from the road to rest on the girl beside him, that sudden smile softened his face. His brows went up in the way she remembered and she was conscious of her heart giving a queer thud.

"I must look perfectly ghastly!" she said. "Lise Brune's clothes don't exactly fit! Her best ones, poor woman! I must see she gets them back quickly."

"She would give you a great deal more than her clothes," said Adrian, "and rightly, I suppose you realise you will be the heroine of the whole village, and the sky will be the limit as far as you are concerned."

"Oh no! Anyone would have done as much."

"I wonder." Although the wetting he had received did not worry him at all, he was suddenly conscious of a cold feeling that had nothing to do with the dampness. He was aware of something else too—that inexplicable desire to protect her of which he had been so acutely conscious on two other occasions.

Changing gear impatiently he shot the big car up the hill.

"You will go straight to bed," he ordered," and I will send something hot, which you will drink and go to sleep."

"Indeed I won't go to sleep! What about Madame?" she retorted indignantly. "And—what about you? Will you—"

"Never mind about me. Do as you are told. As my aunt will certainly order you to."

"But, Mr. Carnforth, I am perfectly all right. It is you who need hot drinks and—"

"Don't argue," he interrupted. "And if you want a quarrel wait until tomorrow."

There was a slight pause, then, "I am hardly likely to quarrel with you—under the circumstances," she said meekly.

He made no reply, and while the silence remained unbroken Sanchia began to realise that she was not going to escape from the reaction of her very unexpected adventure.

It had all occurred so quickly that it seemed almost like something happening to someone else, but now that the need to act was over she knew that it was really herself who had lived through those frightening few minutes in the river. Supposing Adrian had not come? She shivered suddenly, and without taking his eyes from the road her companion asked, "Feeling rotten?"

"Not—very—I shall be all right—really," she replied, hoping desperately that her sudden longing to burst into tears was not obvious.

"No doubt—by tomorrow. Meanwhile I am going to ask Dr. Driscoll to come and have a look at you."

"Oh no!"

Further argument was saved because they were already in sight of the house.

The entrance being reached he brought the car to a halt and before old Jules had time to descend Adrian had opened the door beside his passenger and was helping her to alight.

"Send Celeste to me," he ordered and as the old man

caught sight of Sanchia and positively gaped with surprise at the picture she presented in Madame Brune's anything but perfectly fitting best clothes, "Mam'selle has met with an accident," Adrian told him curtly. "She got very wet. Say nothing to anyone, but send Celeste to me." Then, a hand gripping her arm he guided Sanchia indoors.

Fighting back the weakness which made her long to just lean on him—or on something that offered support, she freed herself, insisting, "I shall be O.K. now. Thank you very much, I—"

But alas for independence! However strong her will power might be, her knees turned to jelly and in spite of a determined effort to reach the safety of the banisters she staggered and would have fallen if it had not been for Adrian who was following.

"Steady." He caught hold of her and for a moment she leant against him closing her eyes. "You are absolutely all in," he told her. "This is ridiculous."

And before she had time to even begin to realise what was happening she felt herself lifted bodily, and was being carried upstairs.

"Oh, please—!" she began.

"Be quiet!" he ordered. "Since you are not fit to go under your own steam, don't be stupid. I'm not abducting you!" In spite of the curtness of his tone she was somehow sure that he was smiling, but she could not see his face because his arm was pressing her so closely. Then all desire to protest died, and—though she hoped vaguely that they would not meet any of the servants—there was something wonderfully comforting about the strength of the arms holding her as easily as though she weighed no more than a baby.

As well as the communicating door from the comtesse's room into the one Sanchia occupied there was another opening directly on to the landing. It was tightly shut when Adrian reached it, and he was faced with the necessity to put down his burden, when a soft voice spoke behind him and a slim dark hand reached out to the door handle.

"Oh, thanks, Mohamed." Without looking round Adrian walked into the room. Though she could not see round him, Sanchia was conscious of a tall white-clad figure moving away with the long soft step she had grown to know so well, and felt that same little *frisson* running down her spine. But she did not know that she had shivered until Adrian asked, "Hello! What's the matter?"

"Nothing," she answered hastily.

"You're telling me," he retorted with unexpected slanginess. "Only a fool would have asked. Time you were between blankets, young woman." Then, in the act of lowering her on to the bed he stopped. "What am I thinking of! You must get out of those clothes. Wait, while I call Celeste." And then she found herself deposited into the armchair.

"But I am perfectly capable of looking after myself now," she protested.

For a moment he paused, looking down at her. Meeting his eyes she saw anxiety in their depths, and something behind it that set her heart suddenly racing.

"My dear," he said in French, "but this is all wrong."

Whether it was the language in which tenderness can be so marvellously expressed, or that the new warmth which she had seen just now was reflected in his tone, she could not tell; she only knew that when he turned abruptly and strode out of the room, an amazing little glow of happiness warmed her.

In an incredibly short time Celeste came bustling in, and exclaiming in horror, had stripped every stitch of clothing off Sanchia, drawn a hot bath and hustled her charge into it. Within a few minutes she found herself

95

powdered, nightgowned, and between blankets, and drinking the hot brandy and water which had arrived via a wide-eyed Marie, while Celeste watched determined that no drop should be left.

"And now," the Frenchwoman announced, her black eyes snapping, "You will sleep until the doctor arrives."

By this time Sanchia knew that it would be useless to say that she did not want a doctor. Anyhow, the brandy and whatever went with it was taking effect, and before she knew what was happening she was sound asleep.

She woke to the subdued sound of voices and looking towards it was puzzled to see Celeste and Adrian by the door. Then in a rush it all came back to her, and with a dismayed exclamation she sat up quickly. "What on earth—?"

"Hello!" Adrian looked round and in an instant was beside the bed, while Celeste followed, ordering, "Keep quiet, Mam'selle."

"Why? I—" Sanchia began.

"Because you must stay where you are. Doctor's orders," said Adrian.

"Doctor's orders? But—"

"Certainly. He will be along again in the morning. Meanwhile he says you are to stay put for at least twenty-four hours longer."

"Oh! but I can't possibly. This is absurd!" she protested, and was cut short again by Celeste's stern, "You must obey, Mam'selle."

"You certainly must," said Adrian firmly. "And those are my aunt's orders also. So don't be obstinate, please."

"I am not being obstinate," she protested. "But what about Madame?"

"Celeste will look after la tante," he told her a little impatiently. Then, his expression softening as he looked down at her, "You will soon be O.K. if you do as you are told. Be a good girl, Sanchia."

Too foolish that the sound of her name on his lips should make her heart behave that way! "It seems— so unnecessary," she said a little breathlessly.

"It is not in the least unnecessary. Really, you should be experienced enough to know that. Anyway, Celeste will see that you are O.K. And I must now report to my aunt." Her hands were outside the bedclothes, and bending down he touched one of them, saying softly, "Don't be awkward, chérie." Then straightening, he nodded to Celeste and went out of the room leaving Sanchia breathlessly aware of the quickening of pulses at throat and wrist, and of seeing the room through a rose-coloured mist of happy amazement. *Don't be awkward, chérie!* Such a simple admonition, but—

Sheer physical exhaustion made it impossible to think further. She closed her eyes, with an unconscious sigh. After all, he was only treating her like a refractory child, and perhaps it was because she felt so stupidly all-in, that she was so ready to like it.

# 8

## I

In spite of Sanchia's protest that she had received nothing worse than a good soaking the doctor still sternly ordered her to rest the whole of the following day. And having passed a bad night broken by terrifying dreams of rushing water she was sensible enough to realise that the warning that she was bound to suffer from a certain amount of shock was right, and Madame who came briskly into her room during the morning, with the aid of a gold-topped ebony stick she used, sat by her bedside and told her blightingly not to be a fool, adding that no one was indispensable.

"I know that," Sanchia admitted meekly. "I am sure that Celeste is looking after you splendidly. But I hate lying up, and it really is not necessary."

"In that case you would not be there. If you *will* try to drown yourself you must take the consequences, my child, and be grateful they are not worse." Though she shook her head disapprovingly, the old lady's voice softened. "I gather that you are now number one heroine of Saint Pierre."

"I never heard such nonsense!" Sanchia protested.

"Nonsense or not, it appears that you fished Lise Brune's son out of the river, and that without your help he would have drowned."

"Anyway, Mr. Carnforth is the real hero. I merely got

cramp and he had to pull me out," Sanchia insisted.

"So I heard, though he did not tell me that," said Madame."

"I don't suppose he would." Sanchia felt her cheeks reddening under the other's intent look.

"What really happened?" the comtesse asked, and when Sanchia explained, "It is fortunate that Adrian was there—that is a treacherous stream. Did you not know that?" Without waiting for a reply she continued, "Anyhow, you are to keep quiet today." She rose, smiling now. "Don't worry, child—I shall do very well." And summoning Celeste who was hovering in the background she took the maid's arm and went away.

In spite of the sleeping pill she had taken, Sanchia passed a second restless night haunted by distressing dreams in which she had been fighting against a raging sea, and just as a hand clasped hers and drew her towards safety Laure Danvers swam up and pulled her back.

Lying in bed now she watched the sunlight making patterns on the opposite wall, wishing that she and everyone else could forget the whole thing. She was getting sleepy when the room door opened and Celeste came in carrying a bunch of roses.

"Jules is getting old and forgetful," the maid murmured. "These should have come with your breakfast tray."

"For me. Oh! how kind. Thank you, Celeste," said Sanchia.

"It is Monsieur Adrian who sent them," replied Celeste. "There is a note."

"Oh—I see." Noticing the rather knowing look Celeste gave her (Heavens! was she also sensing 'romance'!) Sanchia forced herself to sound as if receiving flowers from Monsieur Adrian was a matter of no particular importance. "Please thank him, Celeste," she requested.

"You must do that yourself—when he returns," said

Celeste. Having adjusted the blind and collected an empty glass she lingered asking, "Shall I put the roses in water?"

"Not just now. If you will bring me a vase I will arrange them presently," Sanchia told her a little abruptly.

So Celeste went away, after bestowing another of those understanding smiles on the convalescent. After she had gone Sanchia remained for a brief space looking at the bunch of glowing blossoms lying on the coverlet. So he was not in today! But in any case she would hardly have been likely to see him. Her thanks for his very charming remembrance of her would have to wait until tomorrow. Then she noticed the envelope which had accompanied the flowers and picking it up slit it open with an odd, breathless feeling which she would not have attempted to account for.

She was smiling when she unfolded Adrian's note, but while she read the contents, her smile faded.

Dear Sanchia,

You will be glad to know that the young man whom you clutched back from a watery grave is none the worse for his experience, though you probably won't be so pleased to know that you are almost due for canonisation as a rival saint to Saint Pierre! You will have to wear your halo with becoming graciousness. I am afraid I shall not be around just at present to share the glory. I did not have the chance to mention that I am off to England—only for a few days, I hope, unless complications arise to keep me longer. Meanwhile, please keep out of mischief, and look after my aunt, and yourself!

Au'voir

Adrian.

So she would not be likely to see him again yet. It was curiously disturbing to discover the blank sense of disappointment the knowledge brought. Stupid! But she was too honest not to admit it. She was surprised and dismayed, but it was no use pretending that she had not hoped that what had happened yesterday would have brought them back to the friendly understanding that had begun—and seemingly ended—on their second meeting, and now he had gone away. *And just as well, if you are getting so interested!* Startled by what suddenly seemed a warning inward voice she sat upright, her immediate instinct one of defence.

Of course she was interested; of course she liked him. And now had she not more reason than ever to be grateful to him?

*But have you any right to even hope that he could be interested in you?* demanded that tormenting little voice. None! None whatever—and yet— Half unconsciously she lifted the roses and buried her face in them. After all, he had picked them himself, though, of course, that didn't mean a thing.

Darn! she thought, beginning to be angry with herself, I'd better stop this before I make a complete fool of myself!

An excellent and sensible decision, and one that nothing would have induced her to admit might be just a little too late.


II


In spite of the disapproving noises the doctor made Sanchia managed to overrule his objection and take up her duties again next day.

Though with the exception of her lameness the comtesse was practically back to normal, she did not get up before noon. When Sanchia entered her room she was just finishing her morning session with the tape recorder on to which she always dictated the day's orders for the household. One of her little eccentricities being that it was waste of time to interview the servants.

Looking up she greeted her nurse with one of her most daunting stares and an imperative, "What are you doing here?"

"Good morning, Madame. Until you have finished I will get on with the flowers," answered Sanchia serenely. While she proceeded with the task, Madame switched off the casette and turned to her morning's correspondence. When after a rather lengthy silence Sanchia carried across the big silver bowl of roses on which she had been at work, the old lady looked up, and her nod of approval was accompanied by the unexpected admission, "Very charming." Then, relenting completely, "I missed you doing the flowers yesterday. But I thought the doctor wanted you to rest until tomorrow."

"I didn't need to, and I missed *you*," said Sanchia boldly.

The sudden almost *gamin* grin which this great lady was occasionally capable of, flashed out, but she made no comment. Then touching a letter which she had been reading she said. "Well, we have the house to ourselves. Laure is apparently still enjoying Paris; the good Max is—he alone knows where, while Adrian seems likely to be kept in England, for at least the rest of this week."

Anyway, thank goodness the Danvers were not returning, thought Sanchia. To have to deal with Max's flirtatiousness would have been just too much.

# 9

## I

Both Laure and her husband remained absent during the ten days following Adrian's departure, and since there were no signs of the latter's return, Sanchia concluded that the business which had taken him to England had—as he had suggested it might—kept him longer than it had been his original intention to stay.

Meanwhile Babette Blanchard's fiancé was doing his best to deputise for his boss, and according to Madame, doing very well.

When she looked back afterwards Sanchia realised that although on the surface that week was an uneventful one, by the end of it changes had taken place which made a big personal difference to her. With every passing day her patient grew more independent. Madame, in her nephew's absence, was keeping a determined eye not only on the estate, but on the whole wine business. Every morning Mario came to report to her and she was closeted with him in the room which she used as an office.

But what was most important to Sanchia was a growing understanding between herself and her patient; her increasing discovery that under the decidedly despotic streak in Madame la Comtesse's make-up was an endearing warmth.

Sanchia, always quickly intuitive, very soon discovered

two things: that Madame was always ready to talk of Adrian and that it was he who now occupied the place in her heart which the tragic loss of her only son had left gaping and vacant.

Remembering what he had told her about his boyhood and the school holidays which had always been spent at the château, Sanchia had already realised that Madame's affection was fully reciprocated.

During that week she went driving with the comtesse every day—a new move which the doctor had urged. Though the injured knee was so much better the stairs were still a difficulty. When Sanchia had asked the doctor how Madame was going to get downstairs the comtesse had immediately solved the problem by saying in her peremptory way, "Mohamed will carry me down. He did it when I was laid up before. He'll be useful too if I want to get out of the car. It will give him something to do, instead of hanging about like some faithful hound which has lost its master! He's always unhappy when Laure's away. I must say he's a faithful creature."

And so each day Mohamed sat beside the chauffeur, and because he really was such an excellent servant and seemed so delighted to be of help, Sanchia tried to overcome what she told herself was a stupid prejudice—not very successfully.

After dinner one evening she was sitting with Madame in the latter's boudoir, when her companion startled her by asking abruptly.

"Why don't you like Mohamed, Sanchia?" By now the older woman always used her nurse's first name.

Sanchia looked up quickly from the jigsaw puzzle which she had been helping to put together, embarrassed by the question.

"You do not like him, you know," the other challenged.

"I hope he doesn't know," Sanchia replied, too honest to contradict the statement. "He just gives me the creeps."

"*Ma chère*, why?" Madame demanded. "I confess I was not too pleased when Laure arrived and I found he was part of her luggage. But he is an excellent servant and quite one of the household by now. Anyhow it would have been cruel to send him away. He has been with Laure since she was a child—no doubt a spoiled little brat as children brought up in the East so often are. My brother-in-law left Laure entirely in the care of the woman who was Laure's amah. She was Mohamed's wife and when she died she made him promise he would never leave Laure. All very sentimental, but there it is."

"He is certainly devoted to her," said Sanchia.

"I am sure he would commit murder if she asked him to." Madame laughed, then seeing Sanchia's little shiver exclaimed, "Surely you are not afraid of him?"

Sanchia laughed a little uncertainly. "No. Only he does give me the shivers. Perhaps it is because he always seems to appear when one is least expecting him, and in those white clothes he is like a ghost—and as silent as *revenants* are supposed to be."

"Silly girl," Madame reproved indulgently. "A very solid ghost, and certainly a harmless one."

Sanchia was saved further comment by Celeste's entrance with the evening post, which was always sent up from the village. There were several letters for Madame, and a card for herself with an English postmark and a picture of a lovely East Anglian church on the other side. Surprised, for she could not think of anyone in that particular neighbourhood who knew her present address, and the handwriting was only vaguely familiar, she examined the stamp before reading the brief lines that filled the correspondence space.

> I expect this will be familiar to you.
> Trust all is well. I hope to be back
> in a few days. A.C.

As she read the firm, very masculine handwriting, her heart seemed to turn over.

"Adrian hopes to return in a few days," Madame informed, and then pausing by a table opened a book that was lying on it with the air of someone who is not entirely conscious of what they are doing, shut it again and stared once more frowningly into space. She was so plainly troubled that Sanchia ventured to ask, "I hope you have not had bad news, Madame?"

"Not exactly, but—" She broke off and moving back to her chair resumed the arranging of the jigsaw puzzle again. "At least I can get this right," she said.

It was not until she was alone in her own room that Sanchia remembered that she had said nothing about the postcard which she had received, but she decided that it did not matter, it would mean nothing to the comtesse who had been obviously occupied with what had been in her own letter from Adrian. Had something gone wrong with him? A stab of apprehension shot through her. Then: Whatever happens to him is no business of yours, she told herself, and wished desperately that she could really feel that way. His happiness or unhappiness meant so much more than it should do to her. And he was coming back 'in a few days'. When he came would the emptiness of the house of which she had become so increasingly aware end? But would it not be better if she herself were to go? What a foolish question when she knew it had been there before—too often. That she had thought of him too often. Missed him.

Have I really gone bonkers? she thought. This can't go on. She must either control whatever was happening to her, or go away from here quickly.

You idiot, Sanchia! she thought angrily. Surely you are not going to make that kind of fool of yourself.

Another useless question because she knew the answer

too well. She was not going to make that kind of fool of herself, she had already done it.

## II

Should she find an excuse to return to England? Through a restless night the question remained like a nagging voice at the back of her mind and while she dressed in the morning it was still there.

Always honest with herself, she acknowledged that whatever her mind dictated, her heart was saying a different thing. If she went away she would never see Adrian again; if she stayed—? Well, she would at least be near him, however out of reach he was.

Was he entirely out of reach? Didn't he like her— just a little? It was all very muddled; a foolish jumble to which Sanchia, who had always prided herself on being able to think clearly, could find no real solution.

And this was what happened when a girl suddenly woke up to the devastating fact that her heart had been filched from her by a man who couldn't possibly want it?

Illogical, ridiculous, inexcusable? Probably all of those things, but—true. How little she had dreamed, when she stopped his car and asked a decidedly disgruntled man to give her a lift, what that would lead to.

With a quick, impatient sigh she turned away from the unhappy-eyed reflection in her dressing-table mirror.

When she entered Madame's room she found her already up and wrapped in a dove-grey satin dressing-gown, seated before the small golden walnut writing-desk which she occasionally used.

"Madame! Whatever are you doing up so early?" Sanchia exclaimed.

The old lady turned her head sharply, staring at her questioner almost as though the slender white-clad figure were a stranger.

"Ah! it is you, Sanchia," she said. "I wished to catch the daily post, but—no matter." She picked up the piece of notepaper from the writing pad and tore it into little pieces. "It can wait." But it was clear something had upset her, and connecting it at once with her reaction after reading Adrian's letter last night, Sanchia decided that whatever news he had sent was still worrying his aunt. What could be wrong?

"You have had a bad night!" she said. "Why did you not ring for me?"

"On the contrary, I slept like a top," was the reply. "So well that from the moment I opened my eyes it bored me to lie awake. So I rang for Celeste—it was unnecessary to disturb you. I merely wanted my chocolate and the post. Help me up, *ma chère*, I will go into the boudoir."

Assisting her to rise and putting the ebony stick into her hand Sanchia said, "You hardly need help now—"

"Hardly," Madame agreed. "Ring for breakfast, please." Although she herself kept to the usual coffee, fruit and brioche, the countess had always insisted that her nurse should start the day with a healthy English breakfast.

This morning Sanchia noticed that Madame's own tray remained almost untouched, and that the old lady was unusually silent. She had brought in her morning's mail and she picked up a letter which lay beside her place and read it through very slowly, her face set into an expressionless mask. When she looked up again her eyes were like grey ice, but when Sanchia glanced across the table the set mouth relaxed into a smile.

"Do not look so worried, *ma petite*," she said.

"Was I looking worried?" Sanchia asked. "I was only wondering—but, Madame," she continued quickly, determined to speak while her courage lasted, "I have been thinking more about—about the very little that I can do for you in these days—and—"

"Yes?" prompted Madame.

"You won't be wanting a nurse very much longer. Ought we not to be making arrangements to end my engagement here?"

There was a moment's silence while Madame stared frowning at her. Then, "Does that mean that you wish to return to England?"

"Yes—no. It's just that I feel that I can be of so little further use, it seems unnecessary to remain—" Sanchia stopped unhappily, feeling that she was making a mess of it, and it would end in complete misunderstanding.

"You are bored," said Madame.

"No—oh, no!"

"You wish to go. Tell me truly."

"I don't wish to go, but—if I am of no further use—"

"When you are of no further use," said Madame, "I will tell you." And then, her expression softening, "It is true I may not need a nurse for much longer, *ma petite*. But I shall continue to need a companion. Therefore unless you feel an urgent desire to return to England I would like you to extend your present duties here, until —well, shall we say for another three months. Can you bear to do that?" Then, "Wait!" Madame raised an imperative hand. "If you really desire to leave me—"

"But I don't!" The protest was out before Sanchia could stop it "It was only—" she hesitated. "You have been so kind to me, Madame, if—when I go I shall miss you, but—"

"Tell me. Is there anything that makes you unhappy here. Has there been anything which you have not told me?"

Sanchia felt her cheeks were suddenly flaming, and although to hedge was alien to her she said, "Mrs. Danvers will be returning—and frankly she does not like me."

Madame's face set. "Mrs. Danvers' likes or dislikes do

not run this house," she said, an ice-cold edge to her words. "If she makes you uncomfortable take no notice. In any case there are going to be changes here. My child," she reached a thin white hand out, taking one of the girl's, "I am a difficult old woman, but I am a lonely one. You —however hard it may be for you to understand— have brought a new element here. If I had a daughter I would like her to be like you. I need you here, Sanchia. So don't leave me yet. I will be frank with you. Since I lost my son and my husband, except for one person, my life has been very empty. The only person I could trust is my nephew—I love Adrian and I think he loves me, but though I feel he belongs here he has very deep roots in England and I know I must not tie him. Now the time has come when I must ask him to make a decision—to take on a responsibility he may not want. He is the only person on whose affection I can trust, but we are at the crossroads. I cannot explain now, but I particularly wish you to stay here for the present. Will you do so?"

Puzzled as she was, Sanchia knew it would be impossible to refuse, and it never occurred to her to do so. Suddenly she felt it was not only inclination but duty which urged her to remain for as long as she was wanted. Besides she realised how close these last weeks had brought her to this often formidable old woman, who had just shown a very different side to her complex nature. Her own problem slipping into the back of her mind, she closed her fingers round the hand she held. "Of course I will stay," she promised. "For as long as you want me to."

It never entered her head to wonder what on earth help she could be to Madame as far as the countess's personal problems were concerned. But that was something that the countess had no intention of explaining. When *petit déjeuner* was finished Madame announced that she had an important letter to write and did not wish to be disturbed. They would postpone their morning drive until the afternoon. Interpreting this as dismissal, Sanchia left her and went to her own room after first going downstairs to tell Jules the car would not be needed until later.

After that she found herself at a curiously loose end, and after pottering about her own room for a short time she sat down at the writing-desk which had been installed there, with the laudable intention of sending a rather overdue letter to her cousin which somehow refused to eventuate. After all, what was there to say? In her last brief note Cousin Dorothy had enquired how much longer she—Sanchia—expected her present post to last. Was it not time to come back to England; a friend of hers who ran a home for old ladies—'gentlewomen' Cousin Dorothy explained carefully—was in need of staff. Didn't Sanchia think something like that might be suitable, or was she thinking of taking up hospital work now that she was so much better?

Refraining from replying that that was not the kind of work she wanted, Sanchia broke the news that she would be staying where she was 'for the present', and having written that found it extremely difficult to lengthen out her duty letter and sat staring at it with an odd dismay at actually seeing it written down.

Had she really given her promise to stay here indefinitely? She thought—why had she not found the courage to tell Madame that she must return to England?

I really am behaving like a moonstruck idiot she decided angrily. Why shouldn't she stay? After all, it was up to her to control that errant heart of hers—to get it firmly back in her own keeping.

When they met at luncheon Sanchia noticed that Madame was more silent than it had become her custom to be, and wondered if she regretted having been quite so outspoken. When the time came for their afternoon drive Mohamed appeared as usual to help Madame. There was no need to carry her downstairs now; with the man's strong arm on one side, and the broad balustrade to guide her, she determinedly walked down the long shallow staircase. With equal determination but more ease she finally eased herself into the low back seat of her very beautifully sprung car, which, when her arthritis first showed signs of being really troublesome, had been specially adjusted for her.

Knowing well that in spite of the old lady's valiant ignoring of the escort these preliminaries were bound to damp down her energy, if she remained silent for the first ten or fifteen minutes of their drive, this never worried Sanchia.

This afternoon Madame roused herself very quickly and announced that she had ordered her chauffeur to drive into Nice, where they would have tea before they returned.

It was the first time they had gone so far afield, but though Sanchia wondered if it was not too tiring for the countess she knew better than to make any comment. It was the first change from a completely rural environment she had had since the day—what a long time ago it seemed—when she had so gaily set out on her trip to Grasse—which had ended in such an unexpected way. When the car entered the city it almost seemed as though her former acquaintance with it belonged to some half-forgotten dream, and then while they travelled the length of the Promenade des Anglais she felt again that she was on familiar ground. There was no escaping the fact that though her 'love affair' with Saint Pierre des Montagnes was deeper and different, there was a fascination about this seaside city that had taken, and still held, a piece of her heart.

Today with the sun glinting on the great width of

incredibly blue water and the citadel looking down upon its green height, in spite of the new—or comparatively new—architecture which broke the once very dignified façade of the famous streets, Nice was certainly looking its charming best.

"I am sure you would like to look at the shops, and wander round for a little while," the countess said. "I will put you down by the gardens and pick you up there in half an hour—No, better if you meet me at the Negresco where we can have tea before we return. I have some business to do," she added.

"But—" Sanchia began and broke off, realising that she could not possibly ask how Madame proposed to transact whatever her business was, and how she proposed to go about it.

Seeing her concern the old lady said calmly, "Do not worry about me. Mohamed will look after me."

And so when the car stopped, Sanchia, feeling that for some reason she was not wanted, got out. While she stood on the pavement watching the car drive away she saw Madame lean forward—evidently to direct the chauffeur where to take her, and in a very few moments the Rolls was lost among the press of traffic.

Turning away, Sanchia was conscious of a wave of depression which entirely swamped her happy mood of a short time back. Then she realised that it was not so much an ordinary falling of her spirits as a sudden apprehension of impending trouble, as though the hidden voice which she had heard on more than one occasion in her life, whispered to take care because there was danger ahead.

But what kind of danger?

If only she could have answered that question, but searching for the answer she could only fear that whatever it was would involve Madame.

I ought not to have left her! she thought unhappily.

And then: I am getting morbidly imaginative, I'd better snap out of it.

Nevertheless she had little enjoyment of the shops and the small amount of shopping she did—for things which she had been feeling the want of just lately—because the uneasy feeling persisted until three quarters of an hour later when she arrived at their rendezvous and found Madame ensconced at a table on which tea was already laid.

The countess was looking well and appeared in the best of spirits. While they had tea she chatted gaily. It was so evident that she felt every reason to be pleased with life that Sanchia decided that the odd apprehension which she had felt was just 'a nonsense' due to some physical cause, and by the time they arrived back at the château she had forgotten about it.

# 10

But on the following day Madame appeared to have reverted to her reserved mood and seemed very much occupied by her thoughts. Once or twice during lunch Sanchia caught her watching her with an intentness that was rather reminiscent of the beginning of their acquaintance, and catching her eye on one of these occasions, the old lady shook her head disapprovingly.

"I have been thinking," she said, "it did you good to see some more life yesterday. Since I mean you to remain with me I have no right to be selfish enough to monopolise you—"

"But Madame, you don't," exclaimed Sanchia. "I have all the time I want to myself."

"You have been tied to me for nearly two months now," the countess continued, "and I feel it is essential for you to get at least one clear day a week to yourself," she insisted. "You need more young companionship, and when Adrian returns I shall see that he takes you about sometimes."

"Please don't!" Sanchia exclaimed. "Please—"

"Why? Don't you like Adrian?" was the dismaying demand.

"Yes—of course—I—I should be most ungrateful if I did not realise—how much I owe him." Sanchia found herself stammering, scarlet-cheeked beneath that so reminiscent grey stare. Then pulling herself together she added steadily, "After all, it is not only that he brought me here, if he had not pulled me out of the river I might—"

"My dear child, the last thing that would flatter Adrian is your feeling a sense of obligation to him," said the old lady, half laughing. "For heaven's sake do not let him hear you," she continued, leaning confidentially over the table, "it is as much—more—for his sake than yours that I wish him to be taken out of himself. Between ourselves he has not had a happy time in England and he needs his mind taking off his troubles—I think you get on very well with him and if you can help to keep him cheerful I shall be glad." Then changing the subject abruptly, "Anyhow, you will take this afternoon off. Drive down to the village and have tea at the Inn if you feel like it. I am expecting a telephone call and I have an important letter to write after I have rested."

Since it appeared that she was under orders Sanchia could not argue, though she had already decided not to go down to the village. The truth was she had avoided it since the river episode—she intensely disliked being regarded as a heroine!

And so, telling Jules that she would have her tea brought to her when the time came for it, she took a book and made her way to her favourite spot in the gardens.

There was a small lake which was shut away behind a group of flowering bushes, which were now in full blossom, and as it was away from the main grounds and off the beaten track, having discovered it one day she had got into the habit of walking and sitting there—in the first place because it made it possible to avoid encountering Max Danvers.

But though the book she had brought out was one she wanted to read, somehow it remained neglected in her lap, and she sat watching the waters of the lake, where yellow, blue and pale rose lilies made splashes of delicate colour on the surface. It had been obvious when his letter had arrived that Madame was worried about Adrian. He was unhappy. Things had gone wrong. She wondered what the trouble could be. Something about that house which he so evidently loved and meant to go back to?

To do as Madame wished was not going to help her—Sanchia. If it meant seeing more of him—if he felt obliged to do as his aunt wished—she had made up her mind not to think about him, and here he was—being forced back into her mind—that stupid mind that could not rule her heart.

She wished she had not promised to stay, and felt a swift temptation to write and ask Cousin Dorothy to send a peremptory telegram summoning her back.

That would be letting Madame down. But can I bear to be thrown into closer contact with him? she asked herself. Even if he—likes me a little, won't it only make me more unhappy?

And if she went away and never saw him again—would that make her happier?

I never dreamt this would happen to me! she thought.

But why not? Hadn't she learnt that sooner or later every girl fell in love! Why should she have thought herself immune! But, for once allowing herself to be introspective, she knew that she had known deep down in her that one day she would lose her heart and that when it happened it would be for always, and that was why she had always rejected what she knew to be second-best.

She had waited for the right man—and now—

With an impatient sigh she opened her book. Forcing herself to concentrate she had read half a dozen pages—without, it must be confessed, much understanding of what was on them—when she was dragged abruptly from her effort by a voice exclaiming, "So this is where you've hidden yourself!" and looking round she saw Max Danvers smiling down at her.

For a moment she stared at him blankly. Even if he had been anywhere in her mind, he was the last person she would have expected to see. Had not Madame said that she did not expect him to arrive back yet? But here he was—just about the least welcome person of her acquaintance.

"I say, don't look at me as if I was an unwelcome product from a tall tree," he said. "I assure you I don't crawl—or bite."

"You startled me," she told him. "Good afternoon, Mr. Danvers. I thought you were a long way away."

His narrow eyes regarded her in the way she hated.

Why does he make one feel as if one's clothes were see-through! she asked herself.

"Too far—until yesterday," he said. "And in advance of my lady wife it seems. I rather expected to find her here. When she spoke to me on the telephone last week, she said she expected to be back almost at once. But when I stopped at the Veau d'Argent on my way up I heard that she was still away."

"She is expected tomorrow, or the next day, I believe," Sanchia told him.

"So Jules informs me. How wonderful to find you alone and 'in maiden meditation fancy free'. What were you so engrossed in when I brought you back to earth with such an unpleasant jerk?"

She was saved from answering by the sight of Jules wheeling a tea wagon along the path and glancing quickly at her wristwatch saw to her dismay that it actually was four o'clock already. She rose, saying, "Oh! Jules, I don't think I will have it out here after all. I must go and see if Madame needs me."

"Madame is on the telephone, Mam'selle," said the

butler. "She sent orders that she was not to be disturbed before five o'clock."

"There you are!" exclaimed Max. "But don't send that delectable-looking collection away, out of pity for me—a cup of tea is exactly what the doctor orders. Do tell Jules to bring another cup and let me join you." Though he addressed Sanchia he looked at the butler, who with a murmured "Certainly, Monsieur," went ambling back towards the house. Much as she longed to lose her unwanted companion she felt that she could not just leave him flat, however much she wanted to, and if she insisted on having tea indoors, she would only find herself shut in with him. So, with as good a grace as she could summon, she sat down again, and only then realised that there was no chair for him. Would Jules—who was rather forgetful, think of bringing one?

But Max had no intention of waiting to see; there was plenty of room on the wide seat and edging past the tea wagon he calmly lowered himself into the opposite corner, smiling at her. He had beautiful teeth and not caring how catty the idea was Sanchia decided that he knew it and meant other people to. To be fair he had a rather charming smile, it softened the cynical curve of his mouth and made him look younger. No doubt that smile would get him by with many women she decided, and wondered exactly why she had disliked him from their first meeting.

"My luck's in today," he told her. "I never dreamt I should find you on your own. Are you always free in the afternoons?"

"No, I usually go driving with Madame la Comtesse," Sanchia replied.

"Our dear dragon! And how is she?"

"Very well—a little lame still, but that is more a touch of arthritis than anything left over from her injury."

"As well as that, is she? I hope that doesn't mean you will be taking your departure?"

"Not yet," said Sanchia briefly. "Ah! here comes Jules with another cup." But not with another chair, and again it was difficult to pointedly ask for one. Anyway, thank goodness there was plenty of room on the seat.

Helping himself to a slice of cake and then to a wafer-thin cucumber sandwich, Max Danvers was perfectly aware that his exit would be much more appreciated than his company; knowledge which he found amusing and a challenge. Sanchia had been right when she guessed that the almost professional ladies' man was usually a success with her sex. But however impervious he had seemed to any snubs she had given him in the past he had no illusion about his lack of success with Madame la Comtesse's nurse. From the first her quiet reserve and his complete failure to break through it had intrigued him, and looking at her now he thought suddenly: By Jove, she's attractive! I wonder how far the good Adrian has got with her.

For a few moments he made no attempt at conversation, and in the silence Sanchia tried hard to think of something to say because silences are only possible between people who are in sympathy.

"Well, how does it feel to be a heroine?"

The question was totally unexpected and turning her head quickly she found him studying her intently. "A—heroine?" she repeated.

"Yes. I heard at the Inn that you had greatly distinguished yourself and are now the local Joan of Arc."

She shrugged. "That's only silly exaggeration."

"It didn't sound like it," he told her. "I'm quite shattered not to have been on the spot and the one to help you. Do telll me what happened?" he pleaded. "Madame Brune insists that if it had not been for you some little brat would have drowned."

Sanchia frowned. "I do wish they would forget and not make so much of a trivial thing. Anyhow I had to be pulled out—and that was only because I got cramp."

"But you might have gone under!" He sounded genuinely alarmed. "Who pulled you out?"

Wishing now that she had not mentioned it she answered briefly, "Mr. Carnforth happened to be passing."

So Adrian had been making the running! But it was natural for Max to be sure that no 'normal' man ever wasted time when there was an attractive girl about.

"I see," he said lazily. "Lucky Adrian."

"Did you enjoy your change, Mr. Danvers?" Sanchia was determined to change the subject.

"Some of it—I suppose. Anyhow it was a break. I'll confess," he continued confidentially, "that I'm usually delighted to get away where there are bright lights. This time I rather wished I'd stayed. May I have some of that cake, please, Nurse? I have a childish adoration for cherry cake." That could have been an endearing confession from someone she liked, but she was immune to the schoolboy touch. She cut the cake unsmilingly and handed it to him. Taking the plate from her Max's fingers just brushed hers and, sure that it was not by accident, Sanchia drew a little further behind the tea wagon.

Eating his cake and throwing a few crumbs to a thrush who was hopping about the grass and which gave him a rather old-fashioned look from its bright eyes, Max said laughingly, "I don't believe that bird trusts me."

"You're strange. It's quite tame when I am alone," she replied.

"You come here often then?"

"It's a quiet place to read in."

"My dear, everywhere is quiet," he exclaimed. "Too darned quiet. By the way, where's Adrian?"

"Didn't Jules tell you—?"

"No time to ask—" as a matter of fact he had not thought of doing so. When the butler told him the comtesse must not be disturbed and that Nurse was in the garden he had asked quickly, "Where about in the garden?" and on learning that she was by the lake had come unhesitatingly in search of her.

Seeing that she had finished her tea he whipped out a slim gold cigarette case and opening it held it towards her.

She shook her head. "No thanks. I really must go now."

"No—please!" he pleaded. "Smoke just one with me, then I'll let you escape. It's half an hour before you can disturb Tante Hélène. Come on. Be kind. It's my first day back and I want to talk to you." He had turned to face her at an angle and between himself and the tea equipage she found herself hemmed in. Much as she wanted to go it was difficult to make an issue of it. She decided that it perhaps might be as well to take the opportunity of making him understand that whatever he was after, she was not out for dalliance.

"Very well," she agreed. "But I must go in five minutes."

"There's a sweetie." He lit the cigarette for her, and to her relief moved back to his former position and sat regarding her through the smoke from his own. Then,

"Do you know, I have thought of you quite a lot while I've been away," he told her.

"Indeed?" She sounded obviously uninterested.

"Yes." His deceptively sleepy gaze held hers. "I've been wondering where you could have been all my life? Goodness knows," he said, moving a shade nearer, "one meets few enough people one wants to cultivate. I do hope you don't dislike me too much."

"How absurd you are—"

"Well, you haven't been very friendly. Now, have you?"

he insisted. "You know, I'm rather a lonely kind of chap—"

In another moment, Sanchia thought, he's going to tell me his wife doesn't understand him! "I'm afraid I don't make friends easily," she replied. Then, determined to show him he was wasting his time, "You must have plenty of companionship."

"Me! If it's Laure you're thinking of, we never interfere with each other's—friendships. Look here—I'll lay my cards on the table—I want to know you better." He was leaning forward again now and had moved closer to her. "From the minute I saw you I thought you were the most delightful thing that had happened for years. Why not come and dine with me in Nice one evening—the old girl can't tie you to her all the time—and you must be bored here, unless, of course, I'm trespassing—"

"What on earth do you mean?" Sanchia asked.

"Don't be cross with me—I was just wondering if you and Adrian had—fixed anything."

"I don't know what you are suggesting," she said icily.

"Well, I'd not forgotten he brought you here, and I thought there might be a prior claim."

She stared at him. She had never met an approach like this. Talk about a fast worker—!

"I think you must be crazy," she told him. "But as you are so frank: I have neither the time nor inclination for casual—friendships—and you and I don't speak the same language, Mr. Danvers."

"Come now, you haven't given yourself a chance to find out. But I'm not going to be irrevocably snubbed," he said. "Do come and have dinner one evening—"

"No thank you, really—"

She had risen but as she tried to pass him he caught her hand. "I find you altogether enchanting," he told her. "You delightful little iceberg," and lifting her hand he had put it to his lips before she could snatch it away.

Really angry now, she freed herself and brushing past him almost ran into the arms of the man who was himself in the act of turning back in his tracks.

"I'm sorry—" She looked up expecting to see Jules and with a little gasp of dismayed astonishment found herself staring up into Adrian's eyes.

"Oh! It's you." Aware of her own burning cheeks and the coldness of his expression she thought: He saw! Of course he believed—imagined—she had been having an intimate tête-à-tête with his cousin's husband. Always, always when Max forced his company on her Adrian seemed to appear.

Then true to her training but still too conscious of her blazing cheeks, she controlled herself.

"Oh, Mr. Carnforth! Madame will be so glad you are back again," she said.

"My aunt sent me to look for you." She was sure that it was not imagination that put that cold note in his voice.

"Is she ready for me? I'll go at once." Still conscious of her burning cheeks she hurried away without a glance in Max's direction. She had never been so furiously angry with anyone in her life—what must Adrian think?

Don't be dumb! She told herself contemptuously. Of course he must have seen Max kissing my hand (I wish I'd slapped his face! she thought viciously). But that wouldn't have helped, or stopped Adrian from believing that she must be on very intimate terms with his cousin's husband—or at least of having a good old flirtation in his wife's absence. And wouldn't Adrian know very well that Max wasn't the kind of man who was content with just flirtatious exchanges with a girl who attracted him and who was ready to encourage him, as it must now appear she was?

She felt that the worst feature of the whole thing was that she could not explain; because if Adrian believed her, he would tell Madame and there would be the very devil to pay. In her position how could she make that kind of trouble!

Entering the house she felt tears stinging her eyes. She couldn't go to Madame in this state, her patient was far too shrewd not to see she was upset and insist on knowing why.

Turning her anger on herself, Sanchia decided: And I must be crazy to let myself get in a flap when I'm on duty. If I had not let myself care for Adrian it wouldn't make any difference.

If she did not pull herself together and forget all that nonsense she would have to go, and that was all there was to it. She must write and ask her cousin—who had been against her remaining in France from the beginning —to send her a telegram immediately.

# 11

## I

But three days later she still had not carried out that resolution. There was her promise to Madame; her remembrance of the comtesse's plea to her to remain, and that glimpse of loneliness, of which she had been given such an unexpected sight. True Madame had been very cheerful since Adrian's return, and while he was around there was someone who really cared for her, but Sanchia still found it difficult to write that letter to Cousin Dorothy, which would mean the beginning of the end of her connection with everything to do with Saint Pierre, for she had no illusions, she knew that she would never come back to the little paradise, to the inhabitants of which she had given so much of herself. How perfect it could have been if it had not been for Max Danvers who had certainly played the part of the snake; though his wiles held no temptation for this particular Eve he was still able to poison an environment which might have been quite perfect without him—but not to the extent his wife could—

She was sure anyhow that Max had destroyed any trust Adrian had in her—even any liking.

She had managed to avoid Max since that first day of his arrival—they had only met twice, once on the stairs and then when he was getting into his car and offered her a lift to the village which she refused coldly.

But with Adrian she felt the boot was on the other foot and he avoided any contact with her as often as he could. It was inevitable that they should meet, although those intimate morning visits to his aunt's bedroom had ceased because Madame was now in normal circulation, and he now spent time in the library, the salon, and other downstairs apartments with her.

Apart from the time when they were closeted together discussing estate business, aunt and nephew often walked on the terrace together, and there was no need for Sanchia to hover about her patient. It was when she and Madame were together and he came into the room that she found a difference in his manner towards her; he very seldom stayed more than a few minutes, and although he talked to her it was only to exchange the most conventional remarks, and he always went away as quickly as possible.

Sanchia knew—or thought she knew—that any chance of friendship between them no longer existed. He was disgusted with her because he thought she had been encouraging Max. It was so unfair! But she still felt it impossible to defend herself. In any case it seemed too late to explain. Anyway, how could she possibly reopen the subject? If only she could forget the warmth in his eyes on that day when he had pulled her out of the river and afterwards carried her upstairs! When that foolish little hope that he really liked her had been born.

Facing her aching, secret heart she no longer denied that, without realising what had happened, she had loved him from the beginning.

One morning she was sitting with Madame on the terrace where they were drinking the coffee which Jules always served in the middle of each morning, when the elder woman said abruptly,

"You are looking very pale these days, my child. You must need—" Catching sight of Adrian who was walking along the path below she broke off, calling to him.

He turned, and mounted the short flight of steps leading up to the terrace. "I thought you had gone with Mario," Madame said.

"No. I decided he would manage very well without me," he replied.

His aunt rang the bell on the glass-topped table beside her. "Jules can bring another cup—"

"No—really, thanks. I don't want anything," he told her. "Good morning, Nurse," he added. He always addressed Sanchia as 'Nurse' now, and of course it was plain silly to miss the more familiar use of her first name which he had used so naturally—before he went to England.

"Good morning," she said quietly.

"Did you want me for anything in particular, Tante Hélène?" Adrian asked.

"No. But don't run away," she replied, and when he hesitated, "Sit down and talk to us," she added imperatively. "There is no hurry, surely?"

"I've a mound of paper work," he told her.

"It can wait." Though she sounded dictatorial her smile was affectionate. "Where is Max getting to these days—I suppose he came back so soon because he was broke?"

"I couldn't tell you," answered Adrian indifferently. "Haven't you heard anything of Laure? When does she intend to return?"

"When it pleases her—no doubt. She will probably time it for when her friends return from America and the Château Montpelier opens up."

The house she mentioned belonged to her nearest neighbours. The owner was an enormously rich industrialist who had married into a family who had been famous in the days of the second Empire. Madame had once or twice mentioned them to Sanchia, who gathered that she did not care for them very much. They only spent a short time on their Provençal estate each summer; when they filled the place with guests, and spent the time giving parties and rushing about the countryside in fast cars. Madame disapproved both of their very modern outlook, and their friends.

Adrian agreed drily, "Yes, Laure does not have time to be bored when Simone St. Cyre is in residence. But I hear that Montpelier will not be opened until August this year. Surely Laure does not contemplate staying away as long as that. But have you not heard from her?"

"Laure is a vile correspondent. She writes hurried notes and is sometimes careless about posting them," said Madame. "By the way, Adrian, have you thought anything more about that extension Blanchard wishes to build?"

"Yes, I am going to discuss it with him tomorrow."

While they chatted on, Sanchia, her head turned towards the vista of sunlit gardens, felt suddenly that the blossoming trees, the wooded mountains looking down, the winding white roads; the perfume of flowers—everything she loved about her surroundings, had become just a background for the man who lounged with carelessly unconscious grace in the chair opposite her. He was not looking at her, and she thought with a bitter little stab of pain that she mattered nothing to him. And yet, even while her eyes were elsewhere she was seeing every feature of his sunbronzed profile. The way his thick dark hair grew into a 'widow's peak'—those strongly marked brows and the thick dark lashes fringing the grey eyes—eyes which she was sure would be bleak if he were to turn them towards her. Unconsciously she had looked round herself, and on the same instant he glanced up and their eyes met. For a moment that grey glance held hers, then he gave his attention to Madame again, though not before she had read something new that banished the bleakness she was growing to dread.

It had been an oddly enquiring look; as though he

was trying to find the answer to some question. How could she give him any answer, when she did not know what the question was!

Then she saw that Jules had come out and was approaching Madame, and somehow things were normal again.

"Pardon, Madame," the butler said. "Madame Danvers had just telephoned. She asked me to say that she will be returning tomorrow afternoon, and she sent her love."

Thanking him, Madame dismissed the old man with a nod, and as he went away told Adrian, "There you are. A few minutes ago you asked me when Laure would be back. Talk of—angels!" She was smiling, but Sanchia detected a new hard note in her voice which boded a not altogether cordial welcome for the absentee.

## II

As far as Sanchia herself was concerned the news of Mrs. Danvers' return was unwelcome. She also knew that it made no difference to the acquisitive Max. If he should still be bent on pursuing her unwanted attention to herself, she could hardly appeal to his wife to stop him. But, apart from that, Laure's presence would bring with it a return of the atmosphere of resentful dislike, and that could make for discomfort.

Then Madame spoke again, dragging Sanchia out of her rather unhappy reverie. "Sanchia, would you find the letter which I left on the escritoire in my bedroom, and ask Jules to see that it catches the post? I forgot to bring it down—a long envelope addressed to Monsieur Emil Despard in Paris."

"Of course—I'll get it at once." Glad at least to have an excuse to escape, Sanchia rose.

With the unfailing good manners of his upbringing,

Adrian was also immediately on his feet, and although she did not look up when she passed him, she felt that again he was studying her with that curiously probing scrutiny—but she did not know that for several moments after she had gone into the house he still continued to look after her, while his aunt watched him.

"That girl is having a very dull time, Adrian."

Brought back to recognition of Madame's presence by the abrupt remark, he looked down at her. "Has she not got enough to do?" The answer to that ought to be obvious enough to him, he thought bitterly. Anyway, she seemed to find ways of passing the time! Making it less 'dull' no doubt!

"Sit down," the old lady ordered. "You make me feel a shrimp when you tower like that."

He laughed. "I think I had better go. As Mario won't be back in time I have extra things to see to."

"You are training Mario very well, are you not?" she asked.

"He is extraordinarily capable."

"Um! You meant him to be capable enough to fill your job," she said quietly. "But that must not be necessary, Adrian," and as he was silent and she saw the troubled expression that flitted across his face, she put out a hand, touching his. "I have plans, my dear boy—please do not spoil them. Whatever happens in the future you must always divide your time between here and England."

It was his turn to look troubled. For a moment he regarded her in silence. Then, "I hate to seem difficult," he said. "But you know how it is. Tante Hélène. *Chérie*, I cannot let the old place go, and this chance—"

"It will not be necessary," she interrupted. "You told me that you had until the 20th to make your final decision."

"Yes—"

"That gives you a week. Monsieur Despard is coming

here either tomorrow or Tuesday—I should have seen him before, but since business called him to England and he has been kept there, that was not possible. After his visit things will be entirely altered. I do not want to say more now, because until I have talked things over with him I cannot entirely make up my mind exactly what I mean to do. But, my dearest Adrian, you are in no danger of losing Redleigh—I promise you that."

"But, Tante Hélène," he protested, "what can you do? If you are contemplating any personal sacrifice, I will not accept it, under any circumstances."

"You will allow me to judge the circumstances," she said, her eyes suddenly hard.

"But things cannot change! Dearest, I know you would like to help, but your hands are tied. Even if they were not I could not accept—"

"Will you be quiet, Adrian!" she commanded. "I am not in my dotage, or likely to do anything foolish." Then, her expression softening, she stretched out a hand and laid it on his which were clenched on his knee. "My dear boy, I can only do what in my heart I have always wanted to. Hitherto I have allowed my sense of justice to prevent me following my inclination. I am a firm believer in justice, but it does not always lead along the same path. Mine has been directed into a different channel."

"I'm afraid I don't understand—" he began.

"And you think I am being foolishly mysterious. I do not feel I can explain fully just now. I want Monsieur Despard's advice. After Tuesday I will tell you more— meanwhile I depend on you to leave this business of yours exactly where it is. Will you do that?"

"Certainly, if you wish me to. But I warn you, *chére tante*, I will accept no sacrifice."

"My very dear child, if it were a matter of sacrifice, do you not know I would have made it long ago?" she asked and before he could answer silenced him with an imperative gesture. "No more argument now, please."

Puzzled and not a little concerned, for he felt that whatever scheme she was hatching must fail and disappoint her after she had talked with her solicitor, he rose saying, "I really must get on with some work."

"Very good, but tomorrow I want you to take a day off," Madame announced, "to do something which I very much want you to. Will you?"

Adrian smiled down at her. "A day off?"

"Yes. It will do you good to get away."

"But—"

"Do wait, Adrian! Have you noticed how pale Sanchia is? Not herself at all. She needs change and I want you to give her a break."

"You want *me* to?" He sounded as surprised as he looked.

She nodded. "Yes, and it will be good for you too," she said calmly. "I am running very short of bath oil and those kind of things. The distillerie Cherubin is due to send me a collection of my bath accessories. I want Sanchia to collect a parcel for me. You can drive her over—it will be an excuse to get her out for the day."

He hesitated, on the edge of excusing himself from this very unexpected request, then those expressive brows of his going up, he asked, "And does Sanchia know about this?"

"Not yet. I thought I had better consult you first."

Consult my hat! thought Adrian not quite sure whether to laugh or be annoyed. "Supposing Sanchia doesn't fancy the trip?" he asked.

"Don't be silly. If I want her to do an errand for me, of course she would not think of refusing. Surely you don't mind taking her? Do try to give her a happy time, there's a dear boy. She has seemed rather low-spirited lately, and I particularly do not want her to get so bored that she finds an excuse to leave me."

"What makes you think she would?" he asked quickly.

"She suggested the other day that I do not really need her services any longer, and I feel that I do not want her to go yet. That is why I want you to try to cheer things up for her. She doesn't bore you?"

"Certainly not."

"Very well. It is arranged. Thank you, *mon cher*," his aunt smiled up at him. "Let me tell you something. It will be nice for Sanchia if she is not here when Laure arrives. She knows that Laure does not like her, and I am afraid the knowledge makes her uncomfortable. Reading between the lines I gather that Laure has not been— pleasant. All that must be altered. It will be."

"Good," he approved. "Very well. I will make arrangements for tomorrow."

## III

Back at his desk Adrian left the papers on it untouched while he stared frowningly at the opposite wall. The idea of spending a whole day alone with Sanchia roused mixed feelings in him, some of which he preferred not to analyse. While he was away she had been more often in his thoughts than was conducive to his peace of mind.

Again and again he had relived the sheer horror of that minute when he had pulled her out of the water, and those others, when carrying her up to her room he had learnt in one blinding flash how much she meant to him—that caring for her had only brought a new problem into his life. A problem he half resented because it could divert him from the thing which had always been the single aim to which all his energies must be slanted.

Yet as the days brought him nearer to seeing her again he had looked forward to their meeting with eager anticipation.

And he had found her with Max Danvers! Allowing that swine to kiss her hand, while he—Adrian—was obviously the last person on her mind. He had actually allowed himself to hope that she would have missed him a little and now *he* was the person who was requested to 'amuse' her. Surely she would rather spend a day with the fascinating Max?

Jealous of Max? No—but disillusioned at finding the girl to whom he had given credit for being different to the usual run of her sex in these permissive days, had no scruples over encouraging the amorous approaches of a man like Max.

And I am behaving like some mooning youth who discovers his first beloved idol has feet of clay! Adrian decided cynically.

# 12

It was not until the next morning that Madame informed Sanchia that she wished her to go and collect the parcel that was waiting at the distillery at Grasse where the special perfume which the late Comte had caused to be specially 'designed' for his wife was manufactured. It was a lovely elusive scent, light enough for the daytime, subtle enough for evening use, which characterised all her cosmetics. Madame had told Sanchia that she would never change it. Firstly because it had been her husband's special gift, and secondly because it held so many memories for her.

She said now, "I could get my parcel sent, but I particularly wish you to have the drive—it will do you good. Also," she added calmly, "I want you out of the way today. I do not suppose you will be sad at not being here to greet Laure."

Taken aback Sanchia did not reply for a moment. Then, "But I shall have to meet her, chère Madame," she pointed out, "and I'm afraid she will hate my still being here."

"That is not her business," was the brief rejoinder. "Run away and get ready now, child. I do not want you to keep—the car waiting. Now enjoy your day."

Thanking her, Sanchia accepted her dismissal. She was used by now to the old lady's sudden impulses. Changing from her uniform a few minutes later she realised that she was curiously relieved at the prospect of spending a good part of the day away from the château—and away from the chance of encountering Adrian with what she read as a new cold question in his glance when it rested on her. Spurred by her unhappiness at the complete change in their relationship she was beginning to feel resentful.

After all, surely he should have known better than to condemn her as he so evidently had done! She thought bitterly: *He might have, at least, given me a chance to explain.* Which was slightly illogical, because she knew he would be unlikely to ask her what the little tableau that he had come upon meant, while she herself could never have brought herself to refer to it.

Biting back a sigh, she though, "It's all too stupid. Anyhow it was spoiling everything and wasn't she the fool to let it! Just a weak-minded idiot ever to let herself— like him.

Since yesterday her wish that she had never promised Madame to stay had strengthened, and now she was wondering how much longer she could bear to keep it, for now the hostility between Laure Danvers and herself would inject more poison into the atmosphere. Mrs. Danvers had disliked and resented her strongly enough before she went away, but when she discovered that the objectionable nurse was still here, and noticed—as she was bound to—that Madame was obviously delighted to have her, Sanchia was sure the other girl's jealousy would flare. And that would mean trouble.

In spite of her strict training and her calm exterior, Sanchia had never quite learned to control her sensitive reaction to an unpleasant environment. Though she was ready frankly to own that she disliked Laure quite as much as the other disliked her, she was well trained— and, incidentally, well-bred enough to hide her feelings; and whereas Laure would be out to behave as 'bitchily' as she wanted to, Sanchia could not follow her example.

*In fact a good time will be had by all!* she thought wryly. What with Adrian disapproving of her, and Laure hating her presence in the house—

*Anyway, what a fool I am to care! After all, I've still got a job to do, and so long as Madame is happy what do I care!* she decided with a not very successful attempt at laughing off the threatened situation. At least, with his wife around, there must be less chance of Max resuming his pursuit.

She changed into a blue two-piece, and pulling on a white hat that framed her face with a brim just wide enough to shade her eyes, surveyed the effect with less interest than it deserved. Then turning away from the mirror she took her bag and gloves and went downstairs.

The front door was open, but there was no sign of any car, though she had expected to find it waiting; the elderly chauffeur was usually punctual; as Madame had not explained the arrangement she had made, Sanchia took it for granted he would be driving her and would be there at whatever time he was supposed to be. Jules was not in the hall or his pantry at the back of it, and after waiting for a brief space she turned into the room where she and Madame usually breakfasted, from which she would see her transport when it arrived.

Standing by the window looking out she was aware of the silence of the house. This was the time when the servants would be in their own quarters, except Celeste whom she had seen go into Madame's room as she came out of her own. Seeing the lady's maid Sanchia had thought: Someone else who will not welcome Mrs. Danvers' return with open arms!

Of course Adrian would be busy elsewhere. Adrian! Would she always feel this little stab of pain when she remembered him? And why *must* she remember him, or be hurt because he chose to thoroughly misjudge her?

Her reverie was broken by the sound of a step in the room behind her, and turning quickly she found herself again facing Max Danvers.

"Hello! Hello!" he exclaimed. "This is marvellous! Have you really emerged from purdah?"

"I was not aware that I had ever been in it," she replied.

"Well, slavery then. Our dear tyrant always seems to have you closeted with her. Haven't you any life of your own?"

"I have plenty, thank you, Mr. Danvers." Unconsciously her face had set and the dislike she felt for him was mirrored in her eyes as they met his.

"Don't look so unwelcoming," he begged. "And for the love of Pete don't call me 'Mr. Danvers'! How very formal—I'm Max."

It seemed unnecessary to point out that in spite of the free use by perfect strangers of first names, in these days, she preferred to reserve that suggestion of intimacy for those with whom she was on really friendly terms, and she felt now that she could not have disliked Max more.

"You are looking very delightful this morning," he told her. "I wish you would put away Nurse March oftener; she can be such a very starchy young woman. May I ask if this is her day off, and what *you* propose to do with it?"

"I am going on an errand for Madame," she replied, repressing a longing to tell him to mind his own business, and hearing a car at that moment she would have gone into the hall again, but as she passed him Max blocked her way and catching hold of her arm held her back, laughing down at her, "May I go with you, my pretty maid?"

She had always resented the frank appraisal with which he looked at her, and remembering her last experience with him and the mischief it had made, she felt her blood boil.

"Please let me pass," she demanded. Pierre will be waiting—"

"Let him. And do stop snubbing me!" he exclaimed

impatiently. "I may not get the chance to see you alone again for ages—"

"I believe your wife is returning," interrupted Sanchia pointedly, then, her anger rising, "Perhaps that will give you less time to—waste. Mr. Danvers, I do wish you would understand that I don't like this kind of thing—"

But in spite of her effort to free herself his hand closed more firmly on her arm, while a little flame smouldered behind his lazy narrowed glance. "You know you're absolutely gorgeous when you're angry," he told her.

"Oh! really!" she could not repress an angry little laugh at the sheer banality of the worn-out cliché. "You must have been reading old-fashioned novels. You'll be telling me next that your wife doesn't understand you!"

"On the contrary, she understands me very well. Haven't I told you before, Laure and I go our own ways," he said. "Sanchia, can't you understand that I've fallen for you like a ton of bricks? The moment I saw you I knew that you were something special. Darling, I'm crazy about you—do like me a little."

"You certainly are crazy," she retorted, and as he tried to draw her nearer, "Let me go at once or I shall call for help—I'm sick of this. Can't you realise that I dislike you—and unless you leave me alone I shall be forced to ask Madame for protection. Now let me go."

"I'm damned if I will," he said, his own temper rising. Never before had he experienced this kind of difficulty. However little Sanchia would have believed it in that moment, the handsome Max could usually make easy conquests. He was a born philanderer and to be so determinedly repulsed both annoyed and intrigued him. From the moment he first saw her he had found Madame's young nurse attractive, and far from lessening his interest her determined repulse of him roused all the hunter in him, until he believed that he was really in love with her.

"It's very pretty to play hard to get," he said. "But I'm going to have one kiss before you send me into the night!"

"*Will* you let me go?" She tried again to free herself, but the grip on her wrist only tightened. "Just one, Beautiful—come you can't be mean enough to refuse me that much compensation," he urged.

"No!" said Sanchia furiously. "No!"

"No, no!" he mocked. "Yes, yes, sweetheart—just one!"

"You beast!" Sanchia had never liked being touched, and Max's primitive determination to get his way only strengthened her resistance. But fired by her nearness, he became more eager for conquest. Though he laughed down at her, his eyes were dangerous. "Come, my adorable," he urged thickly. But as he dragged her into his arms she made a fierce effort, and freeing one hand dealt him a stinging slap across his mouth.

"You little fiend!" he exclaimed. "You'll pay me for that! A kiss for a blow, I—" before the kiss could eventuate he was caught by the collar, and with a curse found himself looking up into Adrian's dangerously cold eyes.

"Oh!" With a sobbing gasp of relief Sanchia, forgetting everything else almost ran to her unexpected rescuer.

Facing him and miserably aware of the hardness of his mouth, she said, "As he does not choose to believe me, will you please inform Mr. Danvers that I not only dislike being mauled, but that I despise him more than anyone I have ever met. And will he please understand that unless he stops pestering me I shall be forced to tell Madame that I must go away."

"I shall certainly make that very clear," Adrian's tone was edged with ice, and his hand twisted dangerously in the other man's collar.

"Thank you." Then knowing too well that in another moment she really would burst into tears, Sanchia hurried

141

blindly out of the room and without pausing reached the car waiting at the bottom of the steps.

Seeing it through a mist she only realised vaguely that the nearside door was open and slipped into the seat, not even realising it was the one beside the driver or that the chauffeur was absent. Shaken to the core by the scene she had gone through, she sat biting her lips hard, but almost immediately training won, and though she was still inwardly torn by rage and humiliation she became calm enough outwardly to grope for her bag. Not finding it she bent towards the car mirror. She had straightened her hat and was tucking away a loosened strand of hair when Adrian came out of the house.

"Oh, you are there," he said calmly. "Good. Allow me to restore your property."

"Th—thank you." She took the bag and gloves he held out. He walked round the car and slid behind the wheel. It was only when he started the engine that she became aware that this was the wrong car, and looking round in dismay exclaimed, "I must go back—please! Pierre is to drive me into Grasse and—"

"Wrong," he interrupted. "*I* am driving you to Grasse. By Madame, my aunt's, orders."

"I don't understand," she protested.

"Good Lord!" he glanced briefly round, "didn't she tell you?"

"Indeed she did not."

"How remiss of her."

"But why should you—"

"Wait a minute." His attention was needed to mano-euvre the big open car out into the road, then his eyes still fixed ahead, he said, "For reasons which she has not fully explained she wants to get rid of us both, and so she made the excellent—and true—excuse that you need a day out."

142

"But—I could have gone to the Inn and—talked to Babette."

"I am sure Babette would have been delighted. However, the luck is on my side. If you can bear my company?"

"Of course—I mean——I'm sure you have something better to do, and Pierre—"

"Let's forget Pierre, shall we?" he asked. "And let me apologise for my cousin's husband's behaviour. I don't think you will be bothered again with that kind of thing. I did not know—"

"That I was not encouraging Mr. Danvers' philandering habits." Sudden bitterness welling up in her she looked round at him. "You were under the impression that I enjoyed that kind of thing, weren't you?"

"It was not exactly that—" he broke off finding himself quite unable to explain. How could he say, "I thought you were so different from those young women who enjoy casual affairs, and I hated being disillusioned when I found you obviously on the edge of being kissed by Max." For he knew that it had been something much stronger than his annoyance at believing he had for once in his life been mistaken in his reading of character. After a brief hesitation he said frankly, "I owe you a most humble apology. Can I hope to be forgiven?"

Startled by the unexpected humbleness of his tone, Sanchia found herself at a loss, and there was a moment's silence before she replied.

"Yes. I think so. After all, I suppose it was rather a compromising situation. But I do think that you might have known how unlikely I was—seeing my position in the household—to indulge in that kind of thing, even if I was tempted to—" She stopped realising how stilted and stupid the whole thing sounded. Her head was still turned towards her companion and as he slowed down and looked round again their eyes met.

"I am in sackcloth, Sanchia," he said. "I was a fool.

143

But hang it all! I couldn't very well ask you for an explanation—could I?"

"Why not?"

"Because you would have had every right to tell me to mind my own business."

"It was your business, if you believed I was 'carrying on' with your cousin's husband."

"Hardly. It would have been Laure's business, and she and I are not exactly close enough for me to interfere in her concerns. For heaven's sake! Can't we forget it?" he asked. "This is a lovely day. Don't let us spoil it."

It was a lovely day, and being with him made it much lovelier. The thought might be humiliating but she was too honest to deny the truth. After all, he knew now that he had been mistaken and he couldn't possibly—thank heaven!—know how the misunderstanding had hurt her.

"Please, Sanchia—let's be friends again." He had been travelling slowly and bringing the car to a halt he took a hand from the wheel and touched hers which were lying tightly clasped in her lap.

Feeling that traitor heart of hers leap under the brief impact, she kept her voice steady. "All right, let's forget it. At least you know now—"

"Yes, I do," he said grimly. "So does Max. I have more than half a mind to tell my aunt what has been happening. That would put an end to his residence at le Château Aureoul."

"Oh, please don't," she begged. "I would hate this to cause a family crisis."

"Well, promise that if he makes himself objectionable again you will tell me— I don't think he will, but if he does—"

"I promise that I will tell you," she said quickly.

"Good girl."

From anyone else she might have found the approval

annoyingly condescending, but when he gave her that warm, friendly smile she only felt that life was suddenly worth living again.

# 13

Mrs. Danvers arrived home in the middle of the afternoon. The welcome she received from Jules was correctly polite. Following the old man upstairs her eyes hardened. A day would come when things here were very different, she decided—when these old dodderers would know who was mistress, through the simple fact of being without the responsible jobs which they had retained far too long! But when a little later she found herself alone in her room the set lines of her mouth softened while she looked round the beautiful luxurious apartment.

After all, though the château could be shatteringly boring under the present circumstances, it had its compensations—not the least of which was the knowledge that it would some day be hers. That had always been taken for granted, though she was sure Madame would have preferred a quite different arrangement. The only possible drawback was how much her late uncle had willed her to inherit with the house; she had never been able to find that out, try as she would. But if the worst came to the worst—and she were certain Madame would not be a centime more generous than she was forced to be—she could always sell the place. She had no affection for it, but she rather fancied reigning here, for a time at any rate; entertaining lavishly and living recklessly—surrounded by the kind of people who appealed to her raffish tastes.

Her aunt by marriage had treated Laure with unappreciated generosity at the beginning of her residence; if she had come to feel herself unwanted, that was her own fault—though she would never have admitted it.

Unpacking the small white hide case which contained her cosmetics and other personal necessities a discontented frown shadowed her face. One of the things which she considered she had a right to resent was the lack of a personal maid; the girl who had filled the post before she went away and whom she had taken with her, had walked out on her a few days previously, after her employer had indulged in one of the displays of temper with which she was apt to treat her dependents when she was in the mood. And having failed to find anyone to take Germaine's place, Laure's temper was not improved by having had to rely on herself to do the petty tasks a trained lady's maid would have relieved her of on her journey. Her temper was not improved either by the fact that having thoroughly overspent she had found herself without enough money to travel by air, and had been obliged to make the journey by train—second class at that. The shortage of ready cash from which she periodically suffered infuriated her; she was supposed to keep strictly within the limits of the generous allowance which Madame gave her. But that always vanished all too quickly along with the small private income which was all her father had left her. During these last weeks she had raised every penny she could, but money ran like water through those slender extravagant hands, and now she had no idea how she would manage to pay even enough of the debts she had incurred to keep her creditors quiet.

Re-doing her make-up she was dismayed to note the effect of the crease between her brows. Lines on one's face did not help. Heavens! In a month she would reach her thirtieth birthday—a thing she had always hated the mere thought of. She had an unpleasant feeling that after thirty the years were apt to slip away down the hill to the thing she dreaded—old age! One would have to become quite serious about preserving one's beauty.

What a fool I am! she told herself. After all, I've never failed to attract, and I could be perfectly secure to-morrow if I liked.

In Paris she had seen a lot of King Vernon. She had told him when she expected to be there, and he was more than ready to be at her beck and call. He was crazy about her, and she had made discreet enquiries to ensure he was a rich man. But she had no intention of throwing her bonnet over the windmill for him—or anyone else—while her aunt was alive, and whatever she did with that piece of headgear in the end, she intended to make sure of what she had learnt to take for granted would be her inheritance—if it was only to annoy Adrian. Judging everyone by herself, she was sure that Adrian only stayed here making himself indispensable to the 'old woman' because of what he expected to get out of her. Of course he was a fool to have made his aunt understand so clearly that he cared more for that house in England than for Aureoul, but at least it helped Madame to follow her late husband's wishes about the château, which of course the wine business, now so very successful, would go with.

A soft knock sounded on the door and in answer to her curt permission it opened and Mohamed stood on the threshold making his graceful Eastern greeting.

"Where have you been?" she demanded. "What do you mean by not being here when I arrived?"

"Pardon," the man apologised. "We thought you must arrive on the evening plane. I would have been at the airport if—"

"Since when have you allowed the servants to send you on messages? You are my servant—not theirs. If not you had better leave my service—"

"That I would never do," he replied. "While I live

I serve you. But while you are away I have to belong to this household. I must do what Madame la Comtesse wishes—and it is her will that I make myself useful."

"And you admire the black-eyed Thérèse and run at her bidding," she told him bitingly.

"Those are foolish words, o flower." He spoke as though he were soothing a spoilt child. "I am here to serve you as I promised I would while life was in me."

She turned away with a petulant gesture, and in the silence he watched her, his eyes warm with devotion. He was a proud man, no one else would have got away with treating him as she often did, but from childhood he had adored her. If she had been his own daughter he could not have loved her more.

After an interval she turned towards him again. "Well, what has been happening here?" she asked.

"Mr. Danvers has returned," he replied.

Laure raised her brows and smiling now, repeated, "Well?"

During the next ten minutes she managed to get a fairly clear outline of what had been happening in the household. It would have surprised, but certainly not pleased, the château's mistress if she had gathered what a close scrutiny of the doings, not only of her household, but herself, were noted—but it would have pleased Max even less. Hearing Mohamed's report of her husband's activities, Laure laughed with genuinely pleased amusement.

"I see. So the nurse is not encouraging," she said. And her servant, who had his own set ideas of how women should behave, answered gravely, "He received no encouragement, Madame. The English nurse appears not to like him. She is a well-behaved young woman and a great favourite of Madame la Comtesse."

That was not such pleasing information.

"And Madame la Comtesse is expecting her solicitor," she said.

"So I heard her tell Celeste. It was no doubt to him she sent the telegram from Nice. Celeste told Thérèse that Madame was upset because the gentleman could not come as soon as she wanted him."

"Celeste would not know why he was sent for?"

"No—except that she wanted to give him certain instructions which could not be done by post."

Here Laure seemed to lose interest. "Very well. You can go now," she said. She was frowning thoughtfully as the door closed leaving her alone. Now what had that so-and-so nurse been up to? she wondered. Worming herself into Tante Hélène's favour. Could the old lady have decided to leave her a legacy? The thought of anyone else getting even the smallest portion of Madame's fortune was repugnant to Laure's grasping mind; she adored money and could hardly wait to get those extravagant hands on the portion of it which she had reason to believe one day would be hers. It was bad enough to know what a large share of it would go elsewhere, she thought furiously. And the idea of any stranger being left anything was infuriating. If only—

But this charming train of thought was broken abruptly when the door opened and Max walked in.

"Hello, Laure," he greeted. "You're earlier than I expected. Why didn't you say what time you'd be back?"

"Because I couldn't be sure," she answered. "I came by rail."

"So I gather. Not even a chaste salute to greet your worse half with?" he asked. She offered a cheek, but turning her face with a light touch of his fingers he dropped a brief kiss on her lips. Then catching a full view of her he exclaimed, an odd note of exasperation in his tone, "Gosh! but you're looking marvellous—as usual! Had a good time?"

"Not too bad," she replied indifferently.

"American boyfriend satisfactory?"

She flushed. "Since when have you kept a dossier of my movements?"

He laughed. "Now don't be peevish, darling. It is not a matter of a dossier. We have mutual acquaintances, remember. I happened to have a drink with one of them in Paris and he mentioned seeing you. He was amused at your companion's evident devotion. Mr. King Vernon also happened to be known to him."

"I wish people would mind their own business," said Laure.

"Does it matter?" he asked. "I'm not likely to sue for damages."

"It wouldn't be much good," she pointed out. "No evidence of what I believe our forebears at the beginning of the century referred to as 'crim con'."

"I'm sure of that, darling. You're not exactly generous —or 'trendy' with your favours," he told her. "What a lovely cheat you are! How you get away with it would entirely beat me if I had not learned by experience."

"That is as well, isn't it, my dear?" asked his wife sweetly. But the look they exchanged was not unfriendly. They understood each other very well, these two, an understanding the roots of which were planted in the soil of disillusion.

The attraction that Laure's beauty had held for Max Danvers had soon been quenched by the discovery that under that beautiful, so deceptively feminine façade, the girl he had married was as cold as ice, and that she had only married him because she thought he was a rich man. They had been very nearly on the rocks, and the marriage might have broken up if just a year after their wedding the death of Laure's father had not brought the late Comte d'Aureoul on the scene—the Comte's brother having written before he died to ask him to look after his daughter.

The Danvers had been invited to visit their relatives, and with her usual charm, anyhow where men were concerned, Laure had managed to enchant her uncle who was already a sick man, and even, for a time, to take Madame in.

The result was that the Comte had obtained a promise from his wife that she would look after his orphaned niece and give her a home as long as she needed it. After the Comte's death, Madame, achingly lonely after the loss of her son, then her husband, had been ready to treat the girl as her daughter, until through Laure's own fault the older woman became gradually disillusioned. How deep that disillusion had gone Laure was far from guessing, and with just one slip-up, Laure had continued to play up to her and believe that she was 'getting away with it', though there were certain rules which she knew must be strictly adhered to. She was reminded of the most important of these now when Max said, breaking a brief silence,

"Look, Laure, I want to talk to you seriously." Surprised at his tone she raised her brows,

"What on earth about?"

"Look *chérie*," he said bluntly. "Isn't it time we decided to make a break? I'm not wanted here—"

"Are you mad?" she interrupted. "You know perfectly well how Tante Hélène feels. She is fanatical about marriage. Divorce is something she violently disapproves of. She knows—not being quite a fool—that we are not exactly ideally matched, but she makes it clear that she considers that there is no good reason for our separation. Marriage—according to her belief—is a lifetime institution. So you will have to stick it out while she is alive; after all, you will benefit in the long run." Her voice hardened. "Once the old woman has gone, you can take your share and go your own way. But while she is alive we've got to keep up appearances. Let her believe that we're sticking together."

"But, my dear Laure," protested Max, "this could go on for years. Your expectations are all very well, but in spite of her arthritis—which, thanks to her dear doctor, no longer threatens to cripple her—Madame la Comtesse may live to be a hundred. If you think it's worth waiting for that long, I'm afraid I don't. Supposing I said I'd had the offer of a job—she couldn't very well object to me taking it—"

But the idea did not appeal to Laure. After all, there were times when she found a husband a very convenient background. She said quickly. "You must stick it. You are talking nonsense when you say she'll live to be a hundred. She's not likely to—anything might happen. Why, it was just chance that fall didn't have worse effects."

"That of course must have been disappointing," said Max cynically. "Unobliging of the old lady not to have responded to the treatment, but I'm afraid a loosened stair carpet wasn't exactly effectual, and honestly I don't think you had better try to—hurry things."

"What do you mean?" Meeting his cool glance she paled. "I don't understand what you are getting at."

"Don't you, darling? Anyway, I would rather you laid off that kind of little trick—one must draw the line somewhere, you know."

She began indignantly, "You must be crazy! Are you suggesting that—"

"I'm not suggesting anything. But I am convinced it would take more than a tumble or two to—shall we say —clear the decks? Not a pretty trick, darling. I'm rather a fatalist, and if it is arranged that Madame is to see her century out, *I'm* not inclined to interfere. Besides you may find she is not so anxious for me to stay here."

"Why not?" asked Laure sharply.

Before he could reply there was a tap on the door and

a second later Celeste appeared on the threshold.

"Pardon, Madame Laure," she said, "but Madame la Comtesse has sent me to say she wishes you to take le five o'clock with her. She is waiting for you."

But before Laure had time to consider what this could mean, Celeste disappeared. Max looked enquiringly at his wife, "And what kind of reception do you expect?" he asked.

"Why? I see no reason that it should be anything but pleasant," she replied. "But I mustn't keep her waiting."

When the door shut behind her Max lit a cigarette and stood staring frowningly down at the litter of expensive trifles on the dressing table. He had not been able to bring himself to tell his wife of the scene between himself and Adrian which had taken place that morning. He supposed she would hear about it. Adrian was not likely to keep it to himself he decided, not realising how futile it was to judge Adrian's conduct by the knowledge of what his would have been under the same circumstances.

Perhaps Madame already knew. With a muttered "Damnation," he went across to the windows and stood contemplating the lovely stretch of gardens below without a trace of appreciation. It was true that he was deadly bored with the Château d'Aureoul and everything to do with it, but it was one thing to have left it of his own free will, quite another to find himself 'booted out'.

Of course, Laure wouldn't care two hoots about any affair he had with Sanchia, or any other girl as long as it did not affect her comfort. But if Madame should decide that she wanted to get rid of him and that it was Laure's 'duty' to follow her husband, there would be the very devil to pay. He was annoyed with himself now for not having taken Sanchia's first 'no' for an answer, but hang it all! she was an attractive piece! How was he to know that Adrian was also finding her so?

154

Oh well, he decided, with a shrug, if Laure tore a strip off him he would have to grin and bear it. Anyway he had an idea he might manage to get round the old lady; there had been times when he thought she didn't altogether dislike him, that in fact he rather amused her, and hang it! However broke he had been, he had never tried to touch her for a penny. Like many adventurers, Max was a born optimist, and he decided now that it was no use meeting trouble half way.

# 14

## I

Sitting beside Adrian watching the winding hilly road ahead, though she was still conscious of the little ache which seemed to have taken up permanent residence in her heart, Sanchia was also aware of a new sense of contentment.

After all, was it not easier to take life as it came and be grateful for the moments that helped to make one feel it was worth living? Today she had been given an unexpected break. Any misunderstanding between herself and Adrian was over, he knew now that she was not the kind of girl he had been made to believe she was, and she was here with him—a whole golden day stretching before her. She did not enquire into what Madame's reason for sending them off together was. That seemed the last thing to matter. But having developed a fairly strong inferiority complex, she hoped Adrian was not finding having to bring her out too much of a bind. It did not enter her head that he could really share her pleasure, or that he could be feeling extremely grateful to his aunt.

Though he too kept his eyes steadily on the road ahead, his excellent driving was merely mechanical and his thoughts were very fully occupied with his companion.

Ever since that unfortunate moment on the day of his return, he had been determined to forget all about her, but he had learnt too well how impossible it was. All the time he was in England the memory of this girl had haunted him—a girl who was different from the many others he had met. He had remembered the lovely steadiness of her glance, the curve of her throat, the way her hair grew. Lovely hair that he longed to touch! And half-resentful of the way she haunted him, he had wondered why the dickens he could not forget, when there were other things that were necessary to decide about once and for all.

It was only during the flight back to France that he had reached the stage of asking himself how much Sanchia really meant to him—just exactly what he wanted from her. He had been determined to remain free from complications which he had always been sure would disrupt his life, if he allowed himself to become deeply involved with any girl. Had he at last met the one without whom his life must always remain incomplete? Was he, in fact, really 'in love'? But almost before he asked himself that question he knew the answer to it.

When he had gone in search of Sanchia on his return to the château he had not known quite what he had meant to do about it, and the only thing he was sure of now was that he had made an unmitigated fool of himself. It appeared incredible that he could even have believed she would encourage Max Danvers of all men.

Even now, though, Adrian was not quite ready to admit that such a humiliating emotion as jealousy could have played any part in his belief. Breaking a rather prolonged silence he said, "By the way, I thought, as it is such a lovely day a picnic might be more fun than wasting a couple of hours in a restaurant. When I asked Tante Hélène she agreed. So they've put a luncheon basket aboard for us—but if the idea bores you and—"

"Of course it doesn't," she interrupted. "I love picnics." (Especially for two, when one's companion was the one

157

person in the world she would choose to share it—if she had been given the chance!)

"We will do the errand we've been sent on," said Adrian. "That will bring us to the time when food will be a pleasant anticipation. It will be easy enough to find somewhere where we can unpack our basket—in fact I know an ideal spot. O.K.?"

"It sounds perfect," she agreed, her spirits rising. She suddenly felt an almost childish delight at the prospect before her. After all, why shouldn't she just let herself enjoy every minute of an enchanted interlude without even letting herself think that in a few more weeks at most, it would only be a memory for her and something he would forget.


## II


And so, after collecting Madame's parcel (the contents of which, she already had enough of to last for months!) Adrian turned his car right off the beaten track, and Sanchia finally found herself unpacking the contents of the luncheon basket which the redoubtable Thérèse had stocked with everything that two hungry people—one of whose tastes was decidedly sophisticated—could desire.

"Caviare!" Sanchia exclaimed. "This is certainly a Ritzy meal."

Adrian laughed. "Bless Thérèse! She knows I adore the stuff. I hope there is something here that you particularly like."

"Lobster canapés!" said Sanchia. "Thérèse's specials; oh! and I do believe—yes it is, icecream!" There were enough other delectable eatables to have fed three times the number of picnickers, and though Sanchia had not thought she was hungry, and had only agreed to the announcement that it was time for lunch because she was sure her companion must be starving by now, she discovered that she also had developed an appetite. When she had unpacked the basket, leaving the icecream in its container, they proceeded to enjoy themselves as a couple of healthy young people should. Presently she found herself laughing with the kind of gaiety she had believed she might never be quite capable of again. The secret self-consciousness combined with her certainty that Adrian would never have thought of asking her to come out with him if his aunt had not suggested it, had kept her rather silent during the drive. All that was behind her now while Adrian entertained her with stories of boyhood pranks that had been shared by his cousin.

"He was better behaved than I was," he said, and though he smiled there was a shadow in his eyes. "Altogether a most dependable fellow. God bless his memory! He had the most marvellously happy disposition."

"You miss him a lot," she said impulsively, and bit her lip wondering if she should have spoken.

"Yes—horribly at times. I wish to heaven he had lived —for his mother's sake as well as mine. I hate to think of la tante being lonely."

"She won't ever be that while you are around," Sanchia told him. "I think you have done a great deal towards taking your cousin's place. Madame is devoted to you; and she relies on you completely."

To her dismay she saw him wince, as though from a sudden stab of pain. Then changing the subject abruptly, he began to talk of more impersonal things. By the time they had finished their meal and shared the iced coffee, conversation became desultory until finally complete silence fell.

Always sensitive to atmosphere, her conviction that something was wrong increased, and the inferiority complex which somehow she always fell a victim to where

Adrian was concerned made her once again afraid that she was boring him. Sitting wrapped in his thoughts he seemed to have gone far away.

It was only when she rose softly and began to repack the picnic hamper that he roused himself.

"Do leave that for the present," he said. "I'm too lazy to help."

"There's no need to," she assured. "Anyway you would probably do it all wrong."

"Perhaps you are right! But I do deplore your energy."

She laughed and while she went on with her task silence fell again, until closing and strapping the hamper, she observed with forced cheerfulness, "There you are. All ready, whenever you feel like moving on. What a gorgeous lunch. I am being thoroughly spoilt by all these luxuries."

"No need to move yet, is there?" he asked. "Come and sit down and share my laziness."

"I—don't think we should be too late back," she pointed out. "Won't Madame—"

"For reasons of her own—don't ask me what they are because I haven't a clue—Madame prefers our room to our company today," he said. "Do sit down. I hate people hovering!"

She had paused beside him and reaching out he took hold of one of her wrists, giving it a slight pull. "Sit down, girl."

She obeyed, almost ridiculously relieved, because the touch of impatience was so very much the 'Monsieur Adrian' she knew best. As she lowered herself on to the rug which he had spread earlier he still retained his hold on her wrist. Feeling that it would appear both stupid and prudish to try to free herself, she continued to endure the contact, hoping desperately that he could not feel how her pulse had quickened under his touch. After a moment he released her, asking "Cigarette?"

"No thanks."

He dropped the case he had offered back into his pocket, and to her dismay lapsed into yet another silence. Then,

"Do you know," he told her, "I don't think it would be possible to spoil you."

Startled at the firmness of the announcement she looked round quickly and meeting his eyes found that he was studying her with an interest that brought the swift colour to her face.

"Indeed it wouldn't be difficult." She hoped her laugh sounded natural. "It's been happening for weeks. If I stay with Madame much longer I shall get so used to being feather-bedded that goodness knows how I'll manage my next case. I'm sure it will seem a chore."

Reaching out, his fingers closed lightly on her wrist again.

"Why bother about a next case?" he asked.

"But I must! I've promised Madame to stay a little longer, but as a nurse—as I told her—I am no longer needed. But Madame—" she stopped, feeling it would be a breach of confidence to tell him what Madame had said. Then it seemed that the time had come to regain possession of the hand which he had turned palm upwards and appeared to be studying intently from under frowning brows.

"I wish I could read the future in your palm," he said.

In spite of her effort, this time her laugh sounded unsteady. "I don't think you would find it very interesting," she told him.

"No? What I want to find out wouldn't be in your hand in any case, would it?" With one long index finger he traced the lines of her palm, shaking his head. "It won't tell me when I fell in love with you, or what I am going to do about it."

"Wh—at?" she gasped.

"Oh my darling! Didn't you know?" he asked, and drawing her a little roughly into his arms pressed his lips to hers.

# 15

## I

Was this really happening? Could she have heard aright?

The questions floated vaguely at the back of her mind, but if there had been any answers the loud beating of her heart would have prevented her hearing them. With Adrian's arms about her and his lips on hers she only knew that even if heartbreak and disillusion followed these golden moments they would have been worth the price.

But as the long kiss ended Adrian's clasp slackened and above the turmoil of heart and pulses she heard him say,

"My sweet, I've no right to stake a claim in you and then—just leave you."

"Leave me?" she repeated.

He nodded. "I must go away, darling—quite soon. And is it fair to tie you to me when perhaps I won't be back for years? You see—"

"Yes?" she prompted.

"Do you remember my telling you about my home in England?"

"Yes. That's where you have been, isn't it?"

He nodded. "We must get this straight."

"Yes." Though she felt as though a cold hand had closed on her happiness, she looked at him steadily. "Tell me, Adrian."

And sitting beside her again he tried to explain.

"Redleigh has belonged to the Carnforths for four hundred years. We are part of the soil and it is just part of us, though in a way my allegiance is—I suppose—divided. My mother's blood pulls me to France—my father's to England. Perhaps it is fortunate that I should have to go away from Saint Pierre in any case—but that's neither here nor there. I promised my father faithfully never to let Redleigh go."

But after his father's death he had discovered that the estate was heavily mortgaged. In order to reduce the debt he had let the house and land hoping to go back to it when the lease ran out.

"That was a fool optimist's pipedream," he told her. "For now the mortgagees are threatening to foreclose." He must get the money to save the place. The only way was by accepting an offer to manage the Californian estates belonging to an enormously rich friend of his father's. That would mean that he would be away from England for two years at least, perhaps longer. But the money he earned would save the Suffolk manor."

"And so," said Sanchia quietly, "you have agreed to go?"

"The offer remains open until next week," he said. "My aunt hates the idea of my going, but what else can I do? I promised faithfully."

"Yes."

"So you see, my dearest, that I should not even have told you that I love you. I've no right to mess up your life."

"You had no right not to tell me. If you had just left me to be miserable, believing you never could care for me—do you think that would have been fair?"

"Dearest, you're wonderful!" he told her. "But you must see why I feel it would be criminal to expect you to wait for me for perhaps three years with thousands of miles of sea between us."

"What difference do you think that would make?" she asked. "I would wait for longer than that if you would still want me."

"Want you!" He had moved a little way, and it seemed to Sanchia almost as though the few yards between them stretched into those thousands of miles of sea that threatened to separate them. She thought bitterly how unfair it was when they had found each other for them to be threatened with parting so soon.

"But Adrian," she pointed out, "I—don't quite understand. Madame thinks the world of you. You say she hates the idea of your going so far away. Surely she would help you?"

"If she had the power and if I could bring myself to lean on her," he said. "I never thought I could contemplate doing so, but if it meant saving the unhappiness of parting I know now I might accept help. For my pride's sake I ought to be grateful that with the best will in the world she cannot help me."

"Why not?" Sanchia demanded, too desperate to refrain from the direct question, feeling that her back was against the wall and she was fighting for everything that mattered most in her life.

"Because, although she is a very rich woman she has no power to touch her capital," he replied. "That is yet another complication. When Tante Hélène married him the Comte was a comparatively poor man, and her family tied her fortune—what she had then and what she inherited later—up so tightly that she could not touch a penny of the capital without *her* trustees' consent. The last thing they would agree to would be to her using many thousands of pounds to rescue an English country manor in which her only interest could be that it belonged to the family into which her sister married."

Hearing him Sanchia remembered in a sudden flash that evening when Madame had been so obviously upset by a letter from her nephew and her despairing murmur, *'If only I could help'*.

Drawing her to him again Adrian said fiercely, "Whether you believe me or not, if I was a free agent I would even let the house and everything else go—"

"No!" she interrupted. "You couldn't. You promised your father—I wouldn't let you break that promise, darling."

They had both risen again and turning, she put her hands on his shoulders, looking steadily up at him. "This can't alter things between us. I love you. I would wait forever if I had to."

Perhaps until now he had never entirely escaped from a bitter cynical streak in him—a suspicion born of the unhappy discovery that few people are entirely free of self-interest, but now, with Sanchia's clear steady eyes looking into his so steadfastly, he never doubted that in the girl he loved he had found unfailing loyalty, and the kind of love that would give unstintingly all she had—always.

"I don't deserve you," he said with humility she had never dreamed him capable of.

"Don't dare say that," she flashed, and then, "Darling, I know you will have to go, but," her breath caught a little, "surely you can take me with you?"

## II

While Sanchia and her beloved were still thrashing out the problems that were so vital to them both, Madame was very much engaged with her own arrangements for the lives of certain members of her household.

But her mood had never been more uncompromisingly ruthless, and when she finally called "Come in" to Laure's light tap on the door of her private sanctum there was

166

little warmth in her tone, though her manner appeared very much as usual as she greeted,

"So you have returned?"

"Yes, *chérie*—back again at last, and very glad to be home." Laure kissed the cheek turned to accept the caress. "You are looking marvellous! How's that tiresome knee?"

"I have forgotten it." Madame's eyes, slightly narrowed, searched the younger woman's face. "Hum!" she observed. "You look as though a quiet life would do you good—"

"*Chérie!* Don't tell me I look a jaded wreck." Though Laure laughed, there was a swift vicious gleam in her eyes as she turned away. But she was remembering the famous beauty specialist whom she always consulted when she was in Paris. This time after careful examination she had said tactfully, "Madame has been overtiring herself. With an exquisitely fine skin like yours it is necessary to cherish it." Remorselessly pursuing the point, she added, "Our new cream will help a lot. Especially around the eyes." The label on the appallingly expensive jar said that 'La Crème d'Aphrodite worked miracles on any lines'.

Laure was also forced to remember that an account, with a polite reminder that the three figure total on it was overdue, had reached her before she left Paris.

Those damned bills! and she dare not ask for another penny of her allowance although the old woman was literally rolling in money.

She started and actually coloured beneath her perfect make-up when her aunt said casually! "You must have found Paris expensive. I hope you have not been getting into debt, Laure."

"Of course not." Laure sounded hurt. "Anyhow I didn't need to spend a lot. The American you entertained here, remember him? was staying at my hotel and he certainly returned the hospitality he received here."

"Nice of him," said Madame a little drily and was

silent while she poured out the tea which a maid had just brought in.

Watching the deft movements of those small, surprisingly young-looking hands among the delicate porcelain and shining silver on the big silver tray, Laure was suddenly afraid. She thought, *If she finds out, I'm sunk. Blast her! She can be merciless.* Then, *Don't be a fool!* she thought, *She's not clairvoyant!* She would never guess about that stack of unpaid bills, and after all, she—Laure —had silenced the most pressing creditor—or at least she hoped so, since there had been no reply to her reassuring letter.

With what seemed a complete change of mood Madame chatted away during tea, asking about the American, the plays at the Paris theatres, whether Laure had been to the opera—and what the latest scandals were.

Her niece gave the required information, adding items which she thought might prove amusing and when, tea over, the maid removed the big silver tray and its appendages, she felt that she had done her duty and rose, saying sweetly:

"I'm sure you want to rest now, darling. I'll see you at dinner, won't I? Or do you dine up here?"

"I shall go down tonight," replied Madame. "Wait please. There is something important which I want to discuss with you."

"Yes—?" Laure looked at the speaker, smiling enquiringly. *Now what?* she wondered, but without undue apprehension.

"Yes," Madame told her quietly. "The time has come when it is necessary to make some arrangement about your future."

Crossing the room, she opened a drawer in the small golden walnut writing-bureau standing in one of the window recesses. Watching her, Laure was breathing quickly. The future! Could 'la tante' have made up her mind at last to be more generous? It was over a year now since she had so arbitrarily insisted that her niece by marriage must manage strictly on the quarterly allowance which the younger woman considered utterly inadequate.

*She can't try to reduce it,* she decided. But before she had time to speculate on what could happen now, Madame returned to her seat. She was holding a pale blue oblong envelope and, recognising it as one of those in which she always enclosed her correspondence, Laure realised that it must contain one of the notes which she had sent the old lady during these last weeks.

"Isn't that one of my letters to you?" she asked.

"It is one of your letters," the countess agreed. "I would like you to read it."

Puzzled, and racking her mind in an effort to remember if she could possibly have written anything that could annoy her aunt, and deciding that she most certainly had not, Laure took the closely written sheet of notepaper and glancing down at it caught back a sharp exclamation. *It couldn't be!*

Madame's voice, hard and accusing now, ordered,

"Read it—no doubt your memory will need refreshing."

Laure's eyes slid away from the ice-cool ones regarding her.

"I—don't understand," she stammered.

"You will."

In a few minutes she understood only too well.

"But—Tante Hélène," she stammered, "this—this is not to you—"

"Obviously that was not written to me," said Madame. "You should be more careful, Laure."

Staring down at the sheet of paper, Laure's hand trembled. "You—don't understand—"

"I do, you know. Very well. Indeed, I should be most dense if I did not. If you will read what you have

169

written that will be plain. How very careless of you to put it in the wrong envelope, ma chère."

"But it was never meant to be sent at all—Oh! Tante Hélène, do understand—I was feeling—desperate. I—" she broke off knowing how impossible it was to explain that damning epistle away. How could she have done anything so crazy as enclosing a letter meant for her most confidential friend in an envelope addressed to her aunt!

In the silence Madame bent forward and taking the sheet of paper from her companion's hand began to read, "*Chère—*"

"No, please, please don't," Laure implored.

Ignoring the interruption that inexorable, hard voice continued,

"I am hoping you can help me, as I really am in the most ghastly mess. Simone, *ma chère*, I *must* raise some money. Can you tell me about that man you went to last year—do you think he would lend me, say, two or three thousand pounds, my dear? On my expectations! After all, when the old woman dies I shall be perfectly able to repay—even if she is as mean as ever with the cash, I shall still have the château and the estate—she can't leave that away from me because I am my late uncle's sole next of kin! Of course she will probably live to be a hundred—unfortunately she comes—I gather—from long-lived stock. If only she would obligingly die my troubles would be at an end. Meanwhile do you think your financial friend would lend me the cash? Creditors are worrying me stiff. If the old girl found I was in debt again she would be livid. She wouldn't raise a finger to help. You know she paid up for me before, but only on condition that in future everything was strictly within my allowance. How could I? One must have enough clothes, and they are so appallingly expensive. Now the bank is worrying and won't meet another cheque—while the creditors are descending like wolves.

Do give me helpful advice, and recommend me as a reliable client to your money-lender. I really am desperate.

As Always,

Laure."

Madame raised her eyes, regarding her niece by marriage coolly. "Illuminating, is it not?" she asked.

Laure moistened her dry lips. Every scrap of colour had drained from her face, leaving her beautifully-applied make-up standing out like a mask. What could she possibly say? For once the glibness with which she had so often soothed Madame's annoyance deserted her. In her devious mental make-up there was a very strong strain of sheer stupidity. More than once when she had become involved with some shady transaction Max had straightened (if the word could be used) things out for her. But she had to get herself out of this and decided to obey the not always reliable advice that the best line of defence is attack.

"You must have realised the letter was not meant for you—" she began.

"Why? It began as you sometimes begin yours to me. I am not in the habit of reading other people's correspondence, but I fortunately had read enough to realise how nearly this concerned me before I guessed that it was meant for your friend Madame St. Cyre. However," Madame continued, "that is beside the point. Now, let us sort things out. You believe that if I obligingly died tomorrow you would automatically become the mistress of this house?"

"I—"

"Wait, please. It is sad to disillusion you, but I really cannot help myself."

171

Laure, who had been staring down at the hands which were clasping and unclasping in her lap looked up quickly.

"You can't alter—"

Again Madame stopped her with a gesture. "There is nothing to alter. True, I did at one time contemplate leaving you the château, but I soon had doubts about that which have increased over the years. They are now at an end. On no consideration would I dream of trusting this place to you—"

A stab of fear rousing the angry fighter in Laure, she said tauntingly, "You can't help yourself, *chère tante*—" After all, she thought, it was no use trying to cover up what had happened, and it was a kind of relief not to have to expend her energies on keeping 'the old so-and-so' sweet. It was no use trying to explain away that fateful letter—therefore it was best to come out into the open.

Across these defiant thoughts, Madame's voice came, cold as ice, "That is where you are wrong, my dear Laure. The château is mine, and I am at liberty either to leave directions for its sale, or to put it into the hands of someone whom I can consider worthy of it. I see that you have something to say about this, but let me explain before you waste your energy. In the first place, although your uncle would have liked you to inherit—in the hope that you might have children to come after you—after you arrived here he—shall we say, became doubtful? The way the matter developed makes one of those complicated legal quibbles which are difficult to explain. What finally happened was that the d'Aureoul house and all that goes with it (which, after all, was run by my money after I married your uncle) was legally transferred forever to my estate, and passed right out of the family's hands after Blaise died. Therefore I am at liberty to leave them to whomever I choose—"

"But I have always been led to believe they would be

mine!" cried Laure. "You can't do this to me! I don't believe you can. Of course you want Adrian to have everything—but he shan't! I'll fight through every court in France."

"Don't be silly," advised Madame. "You haven't a leg to stand on, my dear—and on your behaviour your future depends. I will not leave you penniless—as I could quite easily do. I will continue your present allowance and unless some public scandal touches you, I will leave you that same allowance for the rest of your life. You won't starve, though you won't be a rich woman."

"Are you mad?" Laure demanded, staring at her in horror. "I couldn't live on that pittance—"

"No doubt you will find ways of augmenting it," said Madame cynically. "You and your husband are born adventurers—though I will say this for Max, he has never attempted to come to me for more than his keep!"

"But you told me that I was my uncle's heiress—or if you didn't say it in so many words, you let me believe it." Laure sprang to her feet and stood looking down at the older woman, her hand opening and shutting. In these moments all that was worst in her sprang to life. To see the woman who was able to destroy all her ambitions, and her belief in her destiny, sitting there so calmly, maddened her. Then, realising this would get her nowhere she suddenly changed her tune and, dropping on her knees beside Madame's chair, pleaded,

"Please, please believe me when I swear I was off my head with worry when I wrote that letter. I—I hardly knew what I was writing. I know I ought not to have broken my promise but—you don't realise how difficult it is to economise. Everything, but everything, is so desperately expensive, and—and the people I have always dealt with expect me to go on. They encourage one to run up bills and then—"

"I know all about that," Madame interrupted curtly.

"And it is not only your broken word that has made me decide as I have done. I have had enquiries made about you, and certain things have come to light which have forced me to decide to make a fresh will. It is no use, Laure. My solicitor will be here tomorrow and I shall sign the will he has drafted for me. I am not treating you ungenerously. Apart from your allowance I am ready for the last time to settle with your creditors, but only on condition that you and Max leave this house tomorrow."

"Oh no! Where can I go? Tante Hélène," urged Laure frantically, "you can't rob me of my home—"

"It hardly appears that you have appreciated it," was the quiet reminder. "It is useless to argue—my mind is made up. I am paying your debts, and a certain sum will be placed to your credit. No doubt you will spend it, but if you have finally to manage on your allowance, that is up to you. Now please go—and remember, I expect you to leave here not later than tomorrow morning."

Getting to her feet again Laure hesitated—she knew now that it would be useless to try to change Madame's decision—perhaps anyone else would have felt at least a pang of shame, remembering the kindness she had received, the way that since her arrival here, her uncle's wife had poured out money to her, and how she had repaid the generosity with which, in spite of mounting disillusion, Madame had treated her. All Laure felt was hatred and a longing to pour out the abuse that was on the tip of her tongue. But blinded by fury though she was, she had a remaining spark of wisdom reminding her that she could still have more to lose. She had not yet got the money which had been promised to her and the old bitch could change her mind and in the end give her nothing. Better to at least appear to accept her punishment. At the back of her devious, spiteful mind the idea that something might still be done to save herself was vaguely forming.

Without speaking another word she turned and went slowly out of the room.

For several minutes Madame remained sitting very still her hands clasping the arms of her chair. Then a deep sigh escaped her. In spite of the ruthlessness of which she was sometimes capable, she was really very human and at the beginning she had been almost completely taken in by Laure, until the younger woman's shallow selfishness, her insincerity and dishonesty had become only too plain. For a long time she had reminded herself that, however unworthy a one, Laure was a d'Aureoul, though she felt no pride in her name. In fact she took after her mother who had brought scandal and disgrace on the name she had been given. Madame had still hesitated over changing her will. It was only after she read that letter that she was able to definitely make up her mind to have no more to do with the young woman, knowing that her husband would have been in entire agreement with her. And now the next step was to find out how Adrian felt—if he would accept the responsibility she proposed thrusting on him.

# 16

## I

Shut in her own room again—the room whose luxury would so soon cease to be part of her life—Laure paced the floor, her teeth worrying the knuckles of one hand until they drew blood.

She could not even now believe this was really happening. For a time her mind was so chaotic that she found it impossible to think. Then gradually she brought herself to realise what had happened. Something—no matter what—must be done if she was to have any chance of saving herself. Presently she went across to the telephone that stood on her bedside table. On the point of lifting the instrument she drew back, remembering that someone could easily hear what she said, and that it would be better to do her telephoning outside.

As she turned away, all the suppressed rage in her suddenly erupted, and stretching out a hand to the delicate glass powder bowl on her dressing table, she lifted and flung it furiously against the wall. It was part of a lovely set which had been one of Madame's presents to her when she first lived here, and with a sudden determined lust for destruction, she began to treat each piece as she had the powder bowl. It was in the middle of this orgy of hate and destruction that Max came into the room and stood still, staring wide-eyed.

"What the devil's happening here?" he asked.

Jerked out of her blind rage Laure stopped, and looking down at the mess of shattered glass drew a deep breath.

"I'm getting rid of what I don't want, as I am being got rid of," she said.

"What are you talking about?" he demanded. "Really Laure, if you don't learn to control yourself you'll get into real trouble one day. What do you think your aunt will say to this—there must be a couple of hundred pounds worth of Venetian glass there."

"I don't give a damn what she says—I could smash her too—"

"Don't be a fool! What's happened? Have you had a row?" he asked. "It would be so like you to quarrel with your bread and butter."

"I haven't any bread and butter, dear Max," she retorted, pleased at the opportunity to give her husband what she was sure would be the shock of his life. "Neither have you. We are requested to leave here tomorrow—"

"What? Don't be silly! If you've made a fool of yourself you'd better go and apologise," he told her. "What on earth's got into you—don't you know that if you once tread too hard on the old lady's toes she can be more than drastic. I've an idea she has been getting pretty fed up with you, my dear. Better watch your step."

She stared at him. Then she began to laugh, and in another moment he found himself dealing with an attack of wild hysterics.

Curiously he was perfectly able to manage. "Stop that," he ordered. "Do you want to bring the servants in?" And as she opened her mouth to scream, further from self-control than ever, he slapped her face with merciless persistence, first on one cheek, then the other, before he flung the glass of cold water which he produced from the dressing room, right over her.

"You—" she shouted, and then utterly exhausted she

collapsed into a heap of sobbing dampness. Max went across to the door and turning the key turned back to his wife.

"O.K.," he said coolly. "You'll be better presently." And sitting beside her kept a hand on her heaving/ shoulders until true to his prophecy her sobs ceased and she raised her ravaged, now unbeautiful face from the cushions. "And now," he prompted. "What is all this in aid of, my dear?"

She told him what had happened then, and because it would have been useless to keep anything back, told him why.

When she finished he regarded her in silence for a space, and then, "You incomparable fool!" he said softly. "Great heavens above! You don't mean to say you sent Madame la Comtesse the abuse of her—let alone the rest—that you had written Simone?"

She was beyond resenting anything he could say, and she only nodded. "I *can't* think how it happened. I was pretty desperate—but if Simone got Tante Hélène's letter, why didn't she let me know? At least I should have been prepared."

He shrugged. "That's the last thing that matters."

"I know," she rose and going over to the ruined dressing-table found what she needed still intact, and with a horrified exclamation began to repair the damage to her face.

"I believe you've bruised me," she accused.

"Probably. Something had to be done. Did you want Celeste in?"

"Max—" She swung round on him. "What are we going to do?"

"The important thing appears to be what Madame is doing," he reminded her. "Do you really mean we have orders to quit?"

"Yes. And she means it."

He laughed shortly. "Honestly! I can hardly blame her after your very outspoken wish for her speedy demise!"

"I could kill her—Max, do you realise she's going to sign a new will?"

He nodded.

"Well, she mustn't. Do you understand, she mustn't? She must be prevented somehow—I don't care how."

"Don't be dumb, Laure," he advised. "How can you—or anyone else—stop her? She's free, white and can do whatever she likes with her own property."

"Not if anyone had the—the guts to stop her," said Laure. "Listen, Max—it's one old woman between us and practical poverty." She laid an urgent hand on his arm. "We must stop her from signing that will. Surely it is possible to find *some* way—?"

"What way?" Max asked bluntly, adding, "There is no way. You've been a careless fool, and it's no use screaming over the consequences." It was quite unlike him to speak his mind and there was surprise as well as anger in her eyes as they met his unusually steady regard.

"But the 'consequences' affect you too," she reminded him. "What's done can't be undone, but it—can be mended. I tell you, Max, *she must be stopped signing a new will*. Something must be done—"

He shook his head. "No use fictionalising the thing, my dear—this is not a novel where the plot can be manipulated to suit the characters. You've made a mess and we've got our marching orders. I know the old lady—once she makes up her mind nothing will change it—"

She also knew that. Only too well. And stood staring at her reflection in the dressing-table mirror in silence.

Max watched her. Reading her expression he felt a pang of dismay. More than once since their marriage he had discovered a disturbing streak in this outwardly lovely creature. But until Madame had fallen down those steps otuside her apartment he had never suspected how far Laure might go in order to clear an unwanted obstacle from her path.

"I say—" he began.

"Yes?"

"I hope you are not up to any more tricks like that carpet business."

"What are you talking about?" she demanded and then, "What if I am? She's old isn't she? She's had her life—"

"Be quiet!" There was real horror in his eyes as they met hers. "You must be crazy—"

"Not at all. Just determined," she retorted.

"I don't know what devilment you have in your mind," he told her. "You'd better not tell me. Hang it! I do draw the line somewhere, and—I rather like old Madame. She hasn't been too bad to me and I'm quite willing to cut my losses. After all, this frees us, doesn't it? As your aunt has no further interest in you, it won't matter if we part. You will manage better without me—we were married by English law and divorce will be easier than it is in France."

For a moment she was too taken aback to reply. Then, "I see," she sneered, "the proverbial rat leaving the sinking ship. All right. Get out."

"O.K." He moved to the door and pausing there, looked back. "Only don't go too far, because I'm not inclined to be at all helpful."

"Oh, get out," she ordered viciously.

Going to his own room Max began to pack, more disturbed in his mind than he was ready to admit. But presently in his usual careless way he told himself not to be an idiot. Although she was capable of no end of spite Laure was only talking a lot of hot air. There was absolutely no way in which she could stop Madame altering her will, and she was only indulging in wishful thinking if she imagined she could. Anyway, if she chose to get herself deeper into trouble that was her funeral.

But it was a bit steep that after hanging on all these years with the idea that he would participate in his wife's luck when Madame died, the bottom had fallen out of the whole thing. However, there was quite an advantage in knowing himself foot-free. As he had told Laure, he was bored with this place, and after his row with Adrian things would have been—awkward. Pity the pretty nurse had not been of a more coming-on disposition, but there it was. Max had always been ready to cut his losses, and this was his exit.

## II

It was not very long before dinner time when Sanchia and Adrian arrived back. Bringing the car to a halt he exchanged a smiling look with his companion.

"Happy, my sweet?"

"It has been a lovely day," she answered.

"The loveliest in my life," he told her. "However difficult I may have seemed!" Before she could comment on that Jules came out of the house. Adrian had already opened the car door and helping Sanchia out called, "All right, Jules. Don't come down."

"*Oui, monsieur.*" The old butler waited at the top of the steps and going up them Adrian retained Sanchia's hand in his.

Jules said, "Madame la Comtesse wishes to see you, Monsieur Adrian. Shall I tell her you have returned?"

"No. I'll go to her."

As the butler ambled towards his own quarters Adrian looked down at his companion. "Shall I tell her now?" he asked.

She nodded. "Yes—"

"Well, don't look so worried, my sweet," he urged. "Surely you don't doubt that she will be delighted."

But suddenly Sanchia wondered, and when, after bending to kiss her, he ran upstairs she stood watching him until his tall figure faded out of sight on the landing above. Would Madame really be inclined to share their happiness? she wondered with a little twinge of guilt. The thought of the old lady's loneliness cast a shadow on the happiness that had come with the knowledge that she —Sanchia—and Adrian were to belong to each other. If only they did not have to go so far away, leaving Madame here with no one but Laure, who cared only for herself. Madame was not getting younger, and as she had shown Sanchia, she was unexpectedly vulnerable beneath her so often formidable exterior.

Climbing the staircase slowly Sanchia was crossing the gallery towards her own room when a door opened and she came face to face with Max. He was carrying a suitcase and the widely opened door showed her that there was more luggage in the room behind him where opened drawers and wardrobes showed all the signs of hasty packing. Seeing her he stopped.

"Well met! I didn't think I would be lucky enough to see you before I went," he exclaimed as easily as though they were the best of friends.

She stopped, too surprised to do more than stare at him. Then, "Before you go?" she questioned.

"That's right. I'm off. You won't be bothered with me again," he told her cheerfully. "Too bad you didn't like me better, Sanchia—we really might have had fun. Was I an insufferable bore? Forgive me if I was—I don't suppose you will unbend sufficiently to kiss and part friends?"

"Certainly not," she said firmly.

"Oh well—" he shrugged. "Anyhow, wish me luck. I'm starting from scratch again and I'll probably need it." His laugh was suddenly hard. "Well, so long."

"Goodbye."

She had passed him when he called, "Sanchia—"

She turned. "Yes?"

"Look after the beloved tyrant," he said. "She's kicking us out, but I bear her no malice. In fact I would hate anything nasty to happen to her—"

"What do you mean?" Sanchia asked sharply, impressed in spite of herself by a new gravity in his manner. "How could anything 'nasty' happen to her?"

"Just look after her. There might be another loose carpet, that's all. Goodbye." Picking up the case which he had put down he walked to the head of the staircase and ran down it without glancing back.

What on earth—! Puzzled and disturbed, Sanchia continued on the way to her own room. *Another loose carpet.* What could Max mean? And why was he leaving so abruptly? Still speculating about what could have happened while she hastily bathed and changed for dinner, she came to the conclusion that Madame must have heard what had happened this morning. Not from Adrian, there had been no time for that; but could one of the servants have overheard—Jules or even Celeste—and have taken the story to their mistress? She was sure that Celeste would not have hesitated over doing so. Madame's maid detested both the Danvers, and bitterly resented their presence here. It seemed the only possible explanation. But Sanchia had finished dressing before the fact that Max had actually gone away for good sank in—not that it mattered whether he stayed or went now, but what about Laure? With a sudden flash back she realised that he had said "*We* are being thrown out". *We*—that could only mean himself and Laure. It couldn't be possible that Laure was leaving here!

Further speculation was cut short by the arrival of one of the maids bringing a request that she would join Madame la Comtesse and Monsieur Adrian in Madame's boudoir as soon as she was ready.

It took only a few minutes to complete her toilette,

and then, her heart thumping nervously against her ribs and her mouth feeling curiously dry, she knocked on the door of Madame's particular sanctum. In answer to permission she entered the room and almost walked into Adrian.

"Here she is." He put an arm about her drawing her forward.

Madame was seated in a high-backed winged chair, very upright and unsmiling.

'Come and give an account of yourself, Sanchia," she said. "What is this I hear?" Then her expression breaking into a softening smile she held out her hands to the girl. "Come, my dear, and tell me. Is it true—that you and this fellow here have made up your minds to do what I want you to, and get married?"

"What you want?" repeated Sanchia. "Oh, darling Madame, do you really want it?" Kneeling beside the old lady she was gathered into a warm embrace. "Of course I want it," Madame replied, and shaking her head at Adrian, "Have I not made the arrangement in my mind? Only that fellow was so—ridiculously slow. Had to make up his own foolish mind, and now I feel sure you had to help him. You are ready to go a long way away with him?"

"As far as he wants me to," said Sanchia.

"Good, that is how it should be. In love every girl must be a Ruth," approved Madame." 'Thy people shall be my people, thy land my land.' Only fortunately California is not Adrian's land. Though he may have to cut himself in half, at least *half* belongs here." She touched Sanchia's cheek gently, "You, *chèrie*, have a love affair with Saint Pierre and this house?"

"Yes," Sanchia could not keep a little sadness from her tone, "and I will always have, but—"

"That is as it should be," interrupted Madame, "and I hope always will. As far as your fiancé is concerned—

he has promised that he will stay here—"

"Stay—?" Sanchia looked up at Adrian who was standing behind her aunt's chair.

"Yes, darling," he said. "I am staying. Tante Hélène will explain—"

"But not now. I must get ready for dinner," said Madame firmly. "It would take too long to go into details now. Adrian, you have made me very happy—both of you. As you know, I like people to do as I wish them to. What I wish now, Adrian, is that you will tell Jules that we will be drinking the '68 vintage at dinner—there is a celebration."

# 17

I

It seemed incredible that everything could have become so absolutely perfect! Standing by the open glass doors of the library the following afternoon, Sanchia gazed across the flower-bright gardens, feeling that life could not possibly have more gifts for her. Down there, protected by its mountains the village of Saint Pierre nestled, its flat green roofs flooded with sunshine. It was too far to pick out details but she knew it all so well and it made things perfect to know that she and Adrian would spend at least half the year here for the rest of their lives; for that was to be the arrangement. After dinner yesterday evening Madame had explained her plans for her own and their future.

"When I am gone," she had said, "as I have persuaded him to accept the responsibility for my sake, he will be master here and I pray that one day a son of his will carry on—as a son of my lost boy would have done."

So there was no longer any reason for Adrian to go away. Since he was now Madame's sole heir he would have no difficulty in raising the money he needed, and arranging to pay it back later. He would keep his English home, and no doubt be able to live in it later for part of each year.

It was all ideal, and to Sanchia not the least ideal part of it was that Laure Danvers could no longer inject her particular brand of poison into this golden paradise.

Sanchia decided that presently she must go down to the Inn and tell Babette her news—if she did not already know, for every one of the staff here were in possession of the great news that Monsieur Adrian and the Mademoiselle Nurse whom they all loved, were affianced.

Babette herself was going to marry her Mario next month, her parents having been persuaded to remove their objections.

At first Sanchia could not help feeling a little sorry for Laure, but when Madame told her about that letter and the other aspects of Mrs. Danvers' behaviour, even Sanchia's deep fund of compassion for anyone who was down, dried up—Laure had indeed bitten the hand that fed her and deserved whatever might be coming to her when, as seemed inevitable, she had run through the generous lump sum of money her aunt-by-marriage was giving her, and had only her quarterly allowance to manage on.

"But I do not feel we need waste anxiety on Laure," Madame had said. "No doubt she will get rid of Max and marry again—God help the man who gets her."

Laure had left before anyone except the servants were out of their rooms. But Sanchia had seen what had once been the exotic luxury of that bedroom, where the wrecking which had started with the smashing of the Venetian glass dressing-table requisites had been continued with a systematic precision that advertised frighteningly the force of vicious spite behind it. Laure had ripped the brocade hangings and upholstery to pieces and actually sprayed ink and some dark dye over the delicate orchid mauve of the Chinese carpets. It was all so stupid and senseless, but Sanchia sensed a primitive evil behind the wanton destruction that frightened her. The memory of it now fell like a dark shadow between her and the sunlit garden and the sound of a step in the room made her turn with a startled cry, the colour draining from her cheeks.

"What on earth is the matter, darling?" asked Adrian as she ran into his arms.

"Nothing. I thought—" she broke off trying to laugh at herself. "I was remembering Laure's room and—"

"You didn't think she had come back to do some more damage?" he asked. "Really, darling!"

"No—o. But how horrible." Sanchia shivered.

"Childish spite," he said contemptuously.

"I—don't know," she said. "It's frightening. You wouldn't think anyone—especially someone who seemed as sophisticated as Laure—could behave like that. There's such hate in it—" She paled. "Adrian—are you sure she would not try to really harm Madame?"

"Of course not. She took it all out on material things— because I imagine that is what she would have hated to have done to anything of hers. She knows Tante Hélène loves beautiful surroundings and that every room in this house has been lovingly planned—she meant to destroy everything la tante had given her."

"But wouldn't it have been more satisfactory to just take the most valuable away? Doesn't it show a terrifyingly destructive side of her?"

"A rather common vein of spite," said Adrian. "No doubt she throws back to her mother whom I have heard was a dancer in some low cabaret in Budapest, and reputed to have Turkish blood in her. She led her husband a real dance; had a temper like a devil; and finally ran away with one of her husband's Eastern menservants. Not exactly a pretty story, darling, or a very desirable mama for a girl."

"But—did Madame know this?" asked Sanchia, who would hardly have believed what she had heard if it had not been for that wrecked room. To think of the lovely, coolly elegant Mrs. Danvers with anything except aristocratic forebears, seemed completely out of the picture. Then her own second impression of Laure came vividly back to her with the certainty that the other was not only 'bitchy', but capable of real cruelty.

She shivered slightly and when Adrian drew her into his arms clung to him. "My sweet," he said, smiling down at her, "we are going to forget all about Laure and the acquisitive Max, unless of course you want to remember him."

"Indeed I don't," she protested indignantly. And then, her eyes widening, "Max! I have just remembered something he said to me. I didn't take much notice of it at the time, I was too concerned with other things."

He looked at her, his brows going up. "Is it worth remembering now? I cannot imagine Max saying anything really important. What was the brilliant utterance?"

But there was no answering smile on Sanchia's lips. "He was going away, when he came back and said, *'Take care of the beloved tyrant. She's kicking us out but I bear no malice, and I would hate anything nasty to happen to her,'* and when I asked how it could, he said, *'Just look after her; there might be another loose carpet, that's all',* and then he went off. What a fool I was to let him go without trying to find out what he meant. *Another loose carpet*. It's only just come to me! Was—is it possible that Laure had something to do with Madame—I mean Tante Hélène's fall?"

"My sweet, can you see Laure fiddling with bits of carpet?" Adrian asked.

"She could get someone else to do it, and isn't she capable of planning anything beastly? After that room I can believe anything of her. Suppose she tries to injure Madame."

"Darling, this is all a nonsense," Adrian protested. "Laure has gone. Even if she wanted to hurt la tante she won't get the chance."

"But what did Max mean?" Sanchia asked. "Had she made some threat?"

"Probably," he agreed. "But threats break no bones." He stopped as Madame's voice reached them speaking to someone in the hall, then added hurriedly, "Don't say anything to her. She's upset as it is, though she doesn't show it." Almost while he spoke Madame came into the room. She was dressed for outdoors and seeing her Adrian said lightly, "Hello! Where are you gadding off to? Do you want my young woman to go with you?"

"I do not," his aunt replied. "I am going to Nice to meet Monsieur Despard. He has very little time to spare and we can talk business on the drive back."

"I see, wouldn't you like me to drive you, though? I can sit discreetly at the wheel on the way home, while you are tucked in the back seat with the legal boyfriend."

She shook her head decisively. "Certainly not—and do not look anxious, Sanchia—on one is likely to kidnap me on the way. Georges is a very capable young assistant and he is driving me." Pierre, her elderly chauffeur, had gone on holiday that morning, and was visiting his people in Tourraine.

"It's a long drive," Sanchia ventured. "Won't you be very tired?"

"What nonsense! Of course not," Madame retorted. "I am no longer an invalid—I don't need wrapping in cotton wool."

"No. Only—"

"Who told me I no longer required a nurse?" The old lady shook a finger at Sanchia. "Come and see me off, *mes enfants*, and do not *fuss*."

They went out to the waiting car with her and she was driven away waving to them gaily. Sanchia waved back and stood watching the car until it passed beyond the courtyard gates and was hidden by the wall.

As they went into the hall Adrian said laughingly,

"She is right on form again. Nurse March's last and very successful case! What are you going to do without your profession, my love?"

"I shall have plenty to do." But though she smiled at him she found it difficult to ignore the little nagging worry at the back of her mind. She wished Madame was safely back again—or that it was easier to forget Max Danvers' warning. Somehow she was certain that it had been meant as a warning. Why? Now that Laure had gone, who would be likely to wish to harm Madame?

Then, impatient with herself, she decided that she was letting her imagination get the better of her. It was time she stopped.

## II

When, a little later, Adrian, who had things to discuss with his second-in-command, left her, she went in search of old Jules. He was cleaning silver—surrounded by a large collection of exquisite antique pieces. He greeted her with a welcoming smile. Like all the servants he felt a new personal interest in Monsieur Adrian's future wife, and it gave Sanchia a warm glow of happiness to know that though she had been popular with the staff before, she had now become part of the household. She belonged.

It was only when she looked back over the years since her father's death that full realisation of her loneliness came to her. It was still rather difficult to believe that this wonderful thing had happened to her.

"Don't get up, Jules," she ordered as the old man prepared to rise. "I only came to ask you if you knew where Mrs. Danvers was going after she left here."

"Mohamed drove her to the airport, Mam'selle," the butler answered.

"Mohamed? But didn't he go with her?" Sanchia asked quickly.

191

"Yes, Mam'selle, he brought back the Buick and left afterwards in the estate car to catch a train. He had to look after Madame's heavy luggage, I understand Mrs. Danvers has gone to Paris," the butler added.

"I see." She frowned thoughtfully.

"The arrangement was that Georges—the young chauffeur—would go with him in the estate car and bring that back."

"And that happened?"

"Yes, Mam'selle."

"Then Mohamed will be in Paris."

"Yes, Mam'selle."

So they were both out of the way, yet somehow she could not quite rid herself of that vague worry. But Paris —thank goodness—was a long way off; and going presently up to her room she found something new and pleasant in the atmosphere. Now, and in the days ahead she could go about her ordinary affairs without the feeling that there was someone who bitterly resented her presence. It was even more of a relief to turn corners without encountering Mohamed's tall figure coming like some silent ghost, and always disappearing as noiselessly as he had appeared. Whatever she did, Sanchia was sure he would find some way to remain with Laure. There was something touching about his devotion to his idolised employer who, Sanchia was sure, would think no more of turning him away if it suited her to do so, than she would of throwing away a burnt-out cigarette end.

## III

Adrian would be gone now until tea-time, and, taking a book, Sanchia settled down by her window to read. Whether the cause was the drowsy sound of the bees among the flowers below the open window, the warmth of the afternoon, or just sheer contentment, she had not read many pages before she repeated history by doing what she had done on that far off day by the sea when she had missed the bus—she fell sound asleep.

She woke with a start when the book she had been reading slid to the carpet, and consulting her wristwatch she found that it was nearly five o'clock. Tea-time, and Madame must be back.

Tidying herself quickly she arrived downstairs in time to encounter the maid who had served tea, coming out of the salon.

Without bothering to question her Sanchia passed the girl and entering the salon saw Adrian standing by the tall carved mantelpiece. Looking round quickly she realised he was alone.

"Where's Tante Hélène?" she asked.

"Not back yet. She'll be along at any minute. For some reason Marie brought tea in. Jules isn't in this afternoon, but she says he impressed on her not to be late and she didn't know Madame was out."

Marie, a new, young addition to the domestic staff, was rather over-anxious to please and as yet needing more direction than Jules, who was growing sometimes vague with the passing years, realised.

"He probably thought la tante was in, or had forgotten she was out, poor old dear," said Adrian. "There's nothing to prevent us going ahead—I told Marie she must bring fresh tea as soon as the others arrive. They should be here, but I bet they are taking a detour as la tante has so much to say to old Despard. Do the honours, please."

So Sanchia sat down to pour out, and looking up from the task found Adrian watching her, that softened expression in his eyes that had such power to make her heart turn over.

"Darling," he said. "You do look so right there. Such a lovely chatelaine! No wonder I'm told how clever I was to choose just the right girl."

"Who told you that?" she asked.

"The present mistress here—and how right she is. Apparently we have given her the wish of her heart." Then taking the cup she handed up to him, he put it down on the tray and going round the table bent to kiss her. After which he pulled her into his arms, and tea was forgotten.

"*Je t'adore,*" he whispered against her lips. "My darling!" After a few divine moments in which Sanchia, oblivious of everything except the wonder of his nearness and the strength of the arms holding her, lifted her head to search the face above hers.

"When I think of all the years I wasted looking for you," he said lightly, "I wonder how the dickens I got through them."

"You didn't even know I existed," she reminded him.

"But I must have known—in my heart. Wasn't that why no one else would do?"

"There must have been—someone else." It was a very feminine approach, and hearing herself she was appalled. Why ask? Why couldn't she be content with the present? Why delve into the past when what she found there might hurt—though she hoped she was sensible enough to accept that she could not possibly be the first girl in his life.

"No particular 'someone'," he told her. "Shadows, darling—flashing across the screen and vanishing, leaving neither memories nor regrets."

"No one you really fell in love with?"

"Never a one, my sweet. Not after I was seventeen, anyway, when, like the fellow in the song my father was fond of—

I fell in love quite madly
With eyes of tender blue—

She deserted me for another, and after that I became a

hardened cynic at twenty-one!" He did not add: And more and more bored with acquisitive females when the age of the permissive society pushed romantic love out of fashion.

A finger beneath her chin, he lifted her face, "Satisfied?"

"Yes—and dead stupid to want to know," she confessed. "When all I want to be sure of is that you love me."

His lips on hers again answered more convincingly than words, then at a sound in the hall she pushed him away.

"Darling, we must be—sensible. The tea's getting cold."

It is doubtful whether that half-hearted clutch at common sense—and what has common sense to do with lovers?—would have succeeded for long, if the door had not been opened and Marie announced,

"Monsieur Despard."

The small, very dapper gentleman who had followed his name into the room said excitedly, peering shortsightedly towards its inmates,

"Madame la Comtesse, I fear I owe you an apology. I must have muddled my instructions. Perhaps I should have telephoned from Nice when I discovered that you had not come to meet me—"

# 18

## I

"How do you do Monsieur Despard." Adrian moved forward. "My aunt is not here—"

"Not— A thousand pardons! I am ridiculously blind." The little man felt in his jacket pocket and pulling out a pair of tortoiseshell spectacles adjusted them quickly, explaining, "I wore dark glasses on the drive here to protect me from the sun, and I forgot to replace them with my others. Ten thousand pardons."

"Not at all," replied Adrian. "Allow me to introduce you to my fiancée—Monsieur Despard—Miss March. Monsieur is a very old friend of the family, Sanchia, besides being Tante Hélène's trusted adviser."

"I know, I have heard." Then, dropping all effort at conventional politeness, Sanchia asked almost sharply, "Monsieur, is not Madame with you?"

"But no. I expected her to meet me, but she was not at the station." Monsieur Despard looked from Sanchia to Adrian. "I waited, thinking she might have been held up on the way—or perhaps had changed her mind about coming herself, you understand. But no car had been sent. and though I waited almost an hour finally I hired an automobile to bring me here. I tried to telephone but could not get through. Do not tell me that by some error I have missed Madame—"

When Adrian explained that Madame had set out to meet him he looked alarmed.

"But this is terrible. Where is Madame? Can some accident have happened?"

"She certainly went to meet you," Adrian told him. "Was your train late?"

"No. On time to the minute."

"And it arrived at—?"

"Fourteen hours fifteen minutes," supplied the little solicitor.

"But that is three hours ago!" exclaimed Sanchia, then turning her blanched face towards her fiancé, "Even if she decided to wait for the next train she should have been home before this." She clutched his arm. "What has happened? If she never arrived at the station *where is she*?'

It was useless to tell her that there might be some simple explanation, but as pale under his sunburn as she was, Adrian said, "Don't panic, darling. There may be some simple explanation—a breakdown perhaps, which —what's his name? Georges is not so capable of dealing with as Pierre would have been." In spite of his effort to appear optimistic he knew he must sound unconvincing and he exchanged a look with the little solicitor which did nothing to comfort Sanchia.

"Georges!" she exclaimed. "Adrian, do you realise that he was engaged because Mohamed recommended him very strongly. Supposing Laure—"

"My dearest, we won't let our imaginations run away with us. Laure is miles away—she could not possibly have anything to do with—whatever has happened."

"I do not understand," said Monsieur Despard. Then when Adrian explained briefly, "Laure Danvers took a very dim view of my aunt's determination to change her will, and—made trouble."

"So," the lawyer nodded, frowning slightly. "A pity

Madame did not keep the reason for my visit quiet until I was here."

"She was very angry, Monsieur, and determined that the Danvers should leave here."

"Understandable!" Monsieur Despard shook his head. "But naturally there was trouble. I know Madame Laure well. She comes of bad stock, and I am greatly relieved Madame has now made up her mind to be rid of her. However," he half turned to Sanchia, "I do not think she can have anything to do with this. But I fear there may have been an accident."

"Surely by now someone would have been in touch with us if that had happened?" asked Sanchia, and was not comforted when Monsieur Despard pointed out that before a car on the road from the village reached the main road to Nice it was obliged to traverse a very lonely stretch. After all, Saint Pierre was right off the beaten track, as she had discovered for herself. The thought of Madame's car, driven perhaps with some carelessness by Pierre's new young assistant, perhaps lying a complete wreck, added to her anxiety.

But the time for speculation was past, and without waiting another minute Adrian went to ring up the police.

During an interval which seemed to last forever, Sanchia was encouraged by the lawyer who had accepted her right away as one of the family. She told him fully of Laure's rage and its results.

"I cannot help feeling that she might want to injure Madame," she said. "And, Monsieur—I may be unfair but I have never trusted Mohamed."

"The Eastern manservant?" Monsieur Despard shook his head.

"He is devoted to Laure. There is nothing he would not do for her," Sanchia shivered, feeling that too familiar *frisson* which Mohamed always caused. "Madame liked him, but she said that he would commit murder if Laure wanted him to."

Before the lawyer could reply Adrian came back. "It's appalling that police headquarters are not nearer," he said. "It took me an age to get the right person—but apparently there has been no report of an accident though they will make extensive enquiries. But I got hold of Jean Rochard—our village gendarme, and he has gone off to explore the roads between the village and the highway. The Prefect from Nice is coming along as quickly as possible."

And that got them, for tthe time being, not an inch further.

## II

Those next hours were a veritable nightmare, shot through with anxiety and growing fear. One unfortunate feature was that for urgent business reasons Monsieur Despard would be obliged to return to Paris that evening. He had only arranged to spend enough time at the château for Madame to sign her new will and to see that the old one was safely destroyed. This last was something which only Madame herself must do.

It seemed at one point that the house was crowded with policemen. The servants were questioned and re-questioned—and it almost seemed as though every member of both inside and outside staffs were under suspicion of knowing more than they would tell.

Celeste was beside herself with fear for her beloved mistress, and fury that the '*gendarmeie folle*' should dare to think any of her employees could possibly know anything about Madame's disappearance.

Since no sign of the Rolls or its inmates had been found in spite of an intensive search in every conceivable place, the police were beginning to decide this would have to be treated as a case of kidnapping. A couple of months back such a thing had happened not far away. The daughter of a rich American who owned a house in the neighbourhood had been kidnapped while driving alone, and held to ransom.

And Madame was known to be wealthy.

"It is incredible," said Adrian, "that anything like that should happen to my aunt!"

And yet what else could have happened? And then the theory was strengthened by a message announcing that the young man who had been driving the car had been discovered, gagged, tied up and thrown under a hedge.

When he had sufficiently recovered to be able to answer questions his story was that when after leaving the village behind them they reached a particularly lonely part of the road he noticed that the engine was misfiring, and stopping got out to try to discover what was wrong. Madame was in the back, and he was bending down, when he was suddenly seized from behind by an unseen assailant who seemed to have appeared literally out of the ground. All he could remember was a vague impression of some-one tall and enormously strong. Although he struggled desperately, he said, a blow on the head put him right out, and an examination at the hospital where he had been taken, revealed that he had also been drugged. This scanty information was drawn from him in bits, and he was too shocked to be more distinct.

The police were now convinced that this was a matter of kidnapping and another intensive search was started.

There was little sleep for either Sanchia or Adrian that night. To Sanchia the night seemed as though it would never end while she tossed and turned finding sleep or anything resembling rest impossible, until as dawn broke she fell into a short uneasy doze from which she woke with a start and lay wondering why she felt so miserable. Then the reason came back with a rush seeming even more incredible than it had last night.

Remembering the gaiety of the little dinner party at which Madame had celebrated their engagement and how wildly happy she had felt, it seemed too cruel that a devastating thing like this could happen. One read of such things in the newspapers and felt sorry and angry for the victims, but somehow one never dreamt that it could happen in one's own environment.

If only I could do something, Sanchia thought miserably. The idea of Madame in the hands of who knew what criminal types, thrust into sordid surroundings, was almost more than she could bear. Insulted, bullied and frightened until the old lady's splendid spirit broke. But if she had been kidnapped and held for ransom why had no demand been made?

While she was dressing Sanchia was haunted by the fear that Laure could be behind this, and it was useless to remind herself that the other was far away. If she had made up her twisted mind to do mischief, would she not manage somehow?

Adrian came in at the front door just as Sanchia reached the hall. He looked drawn and worried, but brightened at the sight of her. There was no one else about when she ran to him. He took her in his arms, bending to kiss the lips she raised to his.

"Darling." She studied his face anxiously. "Did you get any sleep?"

"Not much, my sweet."

"They think they may have picked up a clue. A black Rolls with the blinds drawn tightly stopped for petrol at a village pump some way beyond Saint Raphael. In spite of the widespread police alert it seems the chap who keeps the garage had not heard about Tante Hélène though even the tiniest, most remote gendarmerie was supposed to have been alerted. Anyway the local fellow didn't warn the garage man until afterwards, and there has been no trace of the car since. Of course there are plenty of that make on these roads. Dozens have been stopped but ours was not among them. I've been with the Prefect, and he assures me everything possible is being done."

The day dragged on with still no news. Adrian was out, scouring the country himself. He would have taken Sanchia with him but she chose to stay indoors, in case the police rang up. To her personal relief, Adrian returned at dinnertime, though the meal, served with all the usual perfection, was sent away almost untouched.

Then when Adrian was urging Sanchia to try to get some rest, the Prefect of Police, who was a friend of Adrian's, telephone to tell him that a message had come through from Cannes. A black Rolls-Royce of the same vintage as Madame's had been found abandoned at a lonely spot in the Alpes-Maritimes; the number plate had been removed, and they would like Adrian to see if he could identify the car. If it was O.K. would he go direct to headquarters at Cannes and he—the Prefect—would meet him there.

"Of course. I will go right away," he said.

When he told Sanchia her heart sank. "But must you go this evening?" she asked. "Surely, if it is only a car—"

"Don't you see, my dear heart, if it should be Tante Hélène's, it will at least give us some clue that she has been taken to that neighbourhood," he said gently. "Please get some rest, my sweet. Why not go to bed early and take a pill or something to make you sleep?"

She shook her head. "I would rather just wait until you come back. You will be back tonight?"

"I hope so. If I'm delayed I'll ring you," he promised. Sanchia had never thought of herself as the clinging vine type, but she had to repress the longing to beg him to stay with her. She was hardly to blame, poor girl; in this welter of fear and misery he seemed the only normal thing left. But, she had been trained to accept crises as part of her life, and she must not fail now! However, she felt she must not make things worse for him.

Yet when he had gone and she knew that she was alone with the servants, she found herself dreading the news Adrian might bring back, and try as she would to fight it her suspicion that Laure was in some way connected with her aunt's disappearance grew into conviction.

They should have tried to get in touch with Laure. Surely, if she was in Paris, the police could trace her movements? Where was Laure really? *Had* she something to do with this?

Those questions haunted her and try as she would to suppress them new fear came to life.

If anything should happen to Adrian now, what would she do? To lose him would be the end of living.

Can't I stop jittering? she asked herself with angry self-contempt. I shan't help anyone if I flap. And she knew that under his calm façade her beloved was almost crazy with worry.

When she had returned after his departure, the house had seemed abnormally quiet. Old Jules was hovering in the hall and seeing her ventured to say, "Mam'selle, you hardly ate anything at dinner. May I bring you something before you go to bed?"

She shook her head. "No, thank you. I shall wait up for Monsieur Adrian. You can leave something on a tray for him, if you like."

With a grateful *"Grande merci, Mam'selle"* the old man had gone away, very relieved at being allowed to do anything. But he left Sanchia feeling that the whole atmosphere was suddenly pregnant with fear. All the senior servants had been with Madame since she came here as a bride, and Sanchia knew that they were now terrified that they would never see their beloved mistress again.

Would they? What had happened to her? Why was there still no demand for a ransom?

## III

Unable to remain still Sanchia rose and began to restlessly pace the room. *If only I could do something*! she thought. Why hadn't she insisted on Adrian taking her with him! Any action would be better than this awful waiting alone.

She was standing by the window staring out into the darkness when the room door was flung open and turning quickly she saw Thérèse on the threshold.

"Mam'selle!" the housekeeper exclaimed excitedly. "You must come with me—you must hear—"

"What is it?" Sanchia demanded. "What has happened?"

"A miracle, but a miracle!" cried Thérèse.

"What do you mean?" Sanchia stared at the woman unbelievingly.

"Come with me and you will know." The housekeeper seized her arm. "Come to Madame's bureau, it is all there!" The woman was almost dragging her towards the hall. "Come," she urged again.

In a moment they had reached the room which Madame had resumed using as a kind of office, from which she directed her management of the household, and also discussed any necessary business with her nephew or Mario.

Shutting the door carefully Thérèse pointed to the wide writing-desk where a small casette stood among the papers littering it.

"It is all there. You know, Mam'selle that Madame dictates her orders for the day. But on Thursday—the day of her so fatal journey to Nice, something went wrong with that machine—"

It appeared that the tape had stuck and Madame had

been obliged to write her order. No one had been into the office since. But this evening when Thérèse had passed the door she had thought that she heard voices. She said,

"For one moment my heart leapt. I thought that by a miracle Madame had returned and was dictating tomorrow's order. Before I had time to think I was in this room, and then I realised the voice came from *here*." She laid a hand on the machine. "But alas! the voice was not Madame's. Listen." She switched the thing on, and after some brief preliminary noises low, urgent tones sounded clearly through the room.

"I have told you what I want, Mohamed. You will bring her to the house where I shall be waiting. It is not easy to find, but—" and then followed detailed instruction of the route which must be taken; the exact whereabouts of a house to which Madame must be conveyed. Obviously the place was right off the beaten track, in the heart of the Alpes-Maritimes near a certain village which Sanchia had never heard of, where Laure proposed to keep her aunt a prisoner until she consented not to change her will. Once or twice Mohamed's deep voice appeared to attempt to interrupt—once it seemed as though he started to protest, but Laure, speaking sharply, told him,

"This is what I tell you to do. If you fail me I shall be ruined. You must not fail—" Then again the dictating machine spluttered, and it was impossible to distinguish the rest of the conversation. While she listened again to the recording which had been unknowingly made by Laure and her devoted henchman, Sanchia knew that the obvious thing to do now was contact the police.

"At once, Mam'selle," Thérèse urged.

"If only Monsieur Adrian were here, he would know the best thing to do," Sanchia cried.

"But, Mam'selle—" the housekeeper began.

"Wait. Don't you see that if the police go along there

Mrs. Danvers would stop at nothing to protect herself. Thérèse—*Madame would not be found.*" Sanchia spoke from frightening conviction, knowing that in a lonely house there were ways of—disposing of someone whose continued existence could bring trouble to the captors.

She said firmly, "I am going to find Madame, and when I have gone you will tell the police. *I* shall make Mrs. Danvers understand that Madame's whereabouts are known and that there is no escape for her. If Madame is safe, Mrs. Danvers can make her escape before the police arrive. She will realise that no matter what she has done, her aunt is never likely to let her be prosecuted. For one thing Madame would never allow the scandal. But I can't waste time talking."

"But, Mam'selle," protested Thérèse, "how will you find this place—how will you even start to get there? There is no one to drive you."

"I can drive myself." Sanchia was determined now. "The estate car is still here. I can drive it. How good at reading a map I am we shall see, but in any case those directions," she motioned towards the tape recorder," are foolproof. I shall copy them down. But there is not time to waste. Tell the police after I have left, and they will be close behind me."

# 19

## I

Driving as swiftly as possible up a road leading into the heart of the mountains, Sanchia realised only too well what risks she was taking. But somehow she hoped that she would be able to convince Laure of the impossibility of using any bluff if the police actually got hold of her. How could she imagine she would get away with this abominable scheme? But then she had no idea that the interview between herself and her servant was being put on the kind of record which allowed no chance of ever disproving it, though for some reason she had decided Madame's office was safer for her interview with Mohamed than any other part of the house—probably when the rest of the household was in bed.

Sanchia had been born with a strong sense of direction, and the Providence which takes note of 'the fall of a sparrow' was with her tonight.

In spite of the intricate route she had to take and the darkness which fell before she was half-way to her proposed destination, she never once missed her way. She had consulted a map before she left, and she knew that on the last few miles she would pass through a village— it could be little more than a hamlet according to its showing on the map. It was completely silent when she drove through, and in the light of the full moon which was now high overhead and flooding the road with its light, the little hamlet looked strangely unreal. Taking a sharp fork of the road she drove on until she came in sight of a solitary house standing back among the trees.

Wise enough not to drive right up to it she ran the car into the shadow of a clump of poplars on the far side of the road, and continued her way on foot. Lights shone from behind drawn curtains. Getting close to the house she walked round the back and found another lighted window on the first floor. Her heart missed a beat. Was Madame there?

*She must be!* she told herself. *She must be!* To believe anything else would have been to waken doubts and shake her resolution.

Going back to the front door she pulled the bell beside it and heard the echo of her summons within. But she had to ring again before, without any sound of footsteps reaching her, the door opened and a tall white-clad figure confronted her.

"Mohamed!" she exclaimed.

She was fully visible in the light beaming out from behind him, and for a moment the man stared down at her, for once in his life utterly at a loss for words.

"I have come to fetch Madame," she said clearly. "Let me in."

As she would have brushed past him he barred her way. "I do not understand, Mam'selle," he said. "Madame is not here—I am alone."

"Oh no you are not," she raised her voice. "You had better bring Madame to me, because otherwise there will be serious trouble for Mrs. Danvers."

"There is no one—" he began, and was interrupted by the opening of a door. A second later Laure walked into the hall.

"Why, it's Nurse March!" she exclaimed. "This is a surprise."

"I am sure it is," said Sanchia curtly. "I think you had

208

better let me in; I have something important to say to you."

"But certainly. Shut the door, Mohamed," Laure drawled. "Mademoiselle has come a long way and we must not be inhospitable. Do come in here, Nurse."

Her heart beating quickly Sanchia followed her and found herself in a luxuriously furnished room where a log fire had been lit against the chilly evenings in this mountain height.

"And now," said Laure turning to face her, her tone changing. "What do you want?"

"I want Madame la Comtesse," replied Sanchia steadily. "You will be wise to bring her to me and let us go away before you make serious trouble for yourself."

"Are you crazy?" the other demanded contemptuously. "Why on earth should my aunt be here? Under the circumstances she could hardly be expected to visit me, or so I should have thought."

"Mrs. Danvers, it is useless to bluff," Sanchia said quietly. "How do you think I found out where you were, and the vile but altogether crazy plan you have made?"

There was no reply. Laure, studying her so very unexpected visitor through narrowed eyes showed no sign of the shock she had received, and after a brief pause, Sanchia continued,

"I came here by *your* directions, and I know exactly what orders you gave Mohamed when you so very unwisely talked to him in Madame's office. You did not realise there was a hidden witness, did you?"

"What nonsense is this? What directions?" Laure demanded contemptuously.

Ignoring the interruption Sanchia repeated, "You never dreamed that every word you spoke was faithfully recorded."

"How could—" Laure broke off beginning to show signs of disquiet for the first time.

"Easily, since the tape recorder Madame uses was in the room, and turned on."

The penny dropped then, and in a flash Laure understood. She drew back instinctively, the colour flooding then draining from her cheeks. "You're crazy."

"Crazy or not, I know Madame is here, and I mean to see her. You will be wise to allow me to take her away, because—" Sanchia stopped, remembering why she had come here alone and what she had said to Thérèse about the police. She was still certain that if the other girl knew that the law was on her track she would find means to get rid of her hostage; to warn her would be to put Madame in immediate danger. *If Madame was still here.* That thought made her sick with apprehension.

Laure had recovered now. After all, what had she to fear? she asked herself. If this fool of a girl wanted trouble she should have it.

Sounding pefectly calm, she agreed. "Very well, my aunt is here, and you can see her. But you had better persuade her to do as I wish. Because—since you know so much—it would be as well to realise that if she still insists on making a new will she will not live to sign it."

"You devil!" exclaimed Sanchia. "You wouldn't dare!"

"We shall see. It is up to her. So you may think it worthwhile to talk some sense into her. Come—" Going to the door Laure opened it and motioning Sanchia to follow, led the way upstairs. There, after crossing a landing and continuing down a long corridor she opened another door. "In here—"

Sanchia moved forward, then seeing that the room was in darkness, stopped. In a split second she felt herself thrust forward, and falling to her knees heard the slam of the door behind her, followed by the sharp click of a key. Then Laure called viciously.

"You will have time to think before the morning, you fool. Stay where you are."

# II

Struggling to her feet Sanchia leant against the wooden panels behind her.

You fool! The contemptuous epithet echoing in her mind she told herself how apt it was.

What had come over her to have allowed herself to be tricked like this, and what would happen now? Would Laure make a complete getaway taking her other prisoner with her? But was Madame still here? The recurrence of that question brought all her fears to life. Why—why had she chosen to come here alone! She tried to comfort herself with the remembrance that Thérèse would not have failed to carry out her instructions—the police must arrive, but it was cold comfort.

Fortunately at this stage she did not know that through an unexpected breakdown in the Saint Pierre telephone service, it had been a full hour after she left before Madame's housekeeper had been able to contact the right people.

# 20

## I

From the way Laure had brought her, Sanchia was certain that this room was at the back of the house and that
it was on this floor she had seen the light. Something told
her that Madame was behind that window. So near and
yet so fearfully far away.

Still keeping her back against the door she spread her
arms out on either side feeling along the walls. Presently
her questing fingers were rewarded. She held her breath
as she pressed down the switch and bit back a cry of joy
as a light flashed on.

If Laure had known there was a live bulb here she
had probably thought that the darkness would defeat
her prisoner, and that she would not find the switch. In
sudden panic Sanchia looked towards the window and saw
to her relief that heavy curtains were drawn across it. This
room—it was a bedroom—had obviously not been used
for a long time. Dust was thick on the furniture and the
carpet, and there was a damp smell about the place.
This was not the time when Sanchia would wonder how
Laure had ever come to be in possession of this house,
or whether the owner of it was also in residence. Her only
thought and desire was to get away and take Madame with
her. But how hopeless that seemed.

It was no use regretting her impulsive behaviour—all
she could do was wait for help to come. Looking down at

her wristwatch she saw with a pang of dismay that it was over two hours since she had left the château. Surely the police should have been here? Supposing they failed to find the place.

Summoning all her common sense she told herself not to be stupid. But she was still terribly afraid of what might happen when they arrived. If only Adrian could have learnt of Thérèse's discovery, she knew that this unexpected delay in the coming of help would not have occurred. And Adrian seemed so far away! Could it be such a comparatively short time since that happy little dinner party at which they had celebrated their engagement! They had all been on top of the world. Would the three of them ever again be happy together?

Presently, after taking her bearings carefully, she turned out the light, in case it showed through some chink under the door. Then she found with relief that a shaft of moonlight came through the drawn curtains and feeling her way towards it drew them back.

When she tried the rusty catch that fastened it—the window opened inward and there was a balcony outside —it refused to move. But by dint of determined manipulation that broke her nails and made one of her fingers bleed, she managed to prise the catch up. The next moment she was feeling air on her face and the window was open.

Listening hard for any sound in the house she waited a few minutes before she stepped outside. A strongly wooded creeper which she recognised at Wisteria, had grown up and over the iron rail of the balcony. The room she had seen when she came round the back of the house and looked up, must be on a level with this one. Creeping softly along, she reached what she was certain must be the window she sought. A light still shone through it and the inside curtains had a gap wide enough to enable her to see right into the room. Hardly daring to breathe, let alone move, she looked in.

The room showed every sign of recent occupation—a tray which had contained a meal of some sort stood on a low table. The room was well furnished and it looked as though some attempt had been made for the comfort of its occupant, but it was empty.

With a pang of bitter disappointment Sanchia remained looking in, then while she stood there, the door opposite her opened and Mohamed came in. He glanced quickly round, then switched off the light. Would he come to the window?

Sanchia slid away, flattening herself against the wall. Five minutes which seemed like five hours passed before she made up her mind the danger was over. She was thinking quickly now. Madame had been in the room and had been taken out of it. What would Mohamed— whom she mistrusted more than ever—do with the prisoner?

I must get help! Sanchia decided desperately. If it was on the way—and what could have happened to delay it— she must meet, and hurry it.

But again how was she to get away? Even if she could have gone back into the main body of the house she would have been at the mercy of those two whom her arrival (Oh! what a fool she had been!) and the knowledge that others beside herself must hear what the tape recorder had to tell, must have made desperate.

Apart from anything else, every instinct of self-preservation warned her to make her escape. With sudden inspiration she lent over the balcony rail, testing the strength of the creeper. Dare she risk going down that way? Then, while she hesitated, the sound of a car's engine reached her, and forgetful of everything she lent over the rail, her eyes searching the direction of the sound —that same direction from which she herself had approached the house. In a few moments she saw the headlights of the large car that was rapidly drawing nearer.

What happened then happened so quickly that she could never remember any details clearly.

Below her, dark-clad figures surrounded the house. A voice called imperatively for admittance in the name of the law; another voice announced, "The door is open!"

Then a light flashed upwards, and still leaning perilously over the balcony Sanchia begged, "Come up to me. They locked me in, and I can't get down."

It was only a matter of minutes before uniformed figures emerged from the room into which she had last looked—where the door had been left unlocked.

"Oh! Why didn't you come before? I believe you are too late," she cried wildly.

There had been unprecedented delay in the delivery of Thérèse's message—someone was going to pay for that. Talking volubly Sanchia's rescuers led her downstairs where the hall was crowded with more policemen.

"You are too late," she repeated, a sob catching the words. "They've gone, and—" She broke off staring up at the staircase where a small, dignified, white-haired figure was slowly descending. Then with a cry of joy she rushed forward.

"Madame!"

"Yes, *ma chère*, I am quite safe," said Madame la Comtesse calmly. "Now don't fuss—"

# 21

"And you mean to say it was Mohamed we have to thank for freeing you?" Adrian looked across at his aunt unbelievingly.

"Yes. You know I always rather liked the fellow," she replied. "But really he treated me quite well, though don't mistake me, my dears, I have no illusions. His over-mastering desire and determination was to save his adored Laure from the punishment of her folly. Of course she should never have been able to persuade him to help her—but I believe that he was speaking the truth when he told me that at first he had no real understanding of the lengths to which she was prepared to go—or make him go. She told him she would be ruined—that I was leaving her without a penny, and he thought—stupid man!——that I could be frightened into doing what she wanted."

"The whole plot was utterly crazy," said Adrian. "She should have known she couldn't get away with it—"

"She might have done, you know," Madame pointed out, "if that machine had not gone wrong. After sticking as it did it must have started again—it has done that before." But Thérèse would have given another explanation.

There was a moment's silence filled with the horror of what might have happened. The sun-filled library where they were gathered on this morning after Madame had returned safely, seemed suddenly dark and cold and Sanchia shivered.

But what Laure had really meant to happen was something that neither then or in the future was ever discussed.

Madame said calmly, "It was a very unpleasant experience, but it is over."

"But, darling, what did Mohamed *say*?" Sanchia could not repress the question.

"He came to me—gave me his 'explanation'! and begged me to forgive Laure. He said—and perhaps he was right—that she had gone a little insane. He implored me not to let her be arrested and said he was taking her away where he could hide her. He asked me to keep out of sight until they were gone and told me Sanchia was in the house and where to find her. But the police came before I could do that." She smiled at Sanchia. "If it had not been for you, *chérie*, things could easily have been different."

"Look, Tante Hélène—Laure can't get away with this," said Adrian furiously. "She's a menace—if she is mad she ought to be locked up."

"No. She has behaved abominably, but she is my husband's niece and that, apart from everything else, forces me to protect her. There will be some difficulty, but I am sure Monsieur Despard will do as I wish and—let things remain as they are," said Madame. "She will be leaving France—my suggestion is that she should go East again and stay there." She did not add that she had made her arrangement with Mohamed and was providing the money for Laure's perpetual exile—while her allowance would only be paid on the understanding that she remained abroad.

"Well, it is over. Let us try to forget it." Madame rose. "Sanchia, you look pale. You are in need of rest, and I have promised Celeste that I will take things very quietly today. See your young woman does the same, Adrian."

"And please do as Celeste wishes, or I shall have to be your nurse again," Sanchia told her.

"That is, as you English are fond of saying, 'a nonsense'," said Madame.

She was going out of the room while Adrian held the door open for her, when Sanchia said quickly, "Tante Hélène—do you—I suppose you don't know how Laure came to be in possession of that house?"

The comtesse stopped, looking round. "Oh yes, Mohamed told me. It belongs to her great friend, Simone St. Cyre, and her husband Blaise, who are having it altered and redecorated. They will use it as a shooting box. It appears that Laure was to advise on the decoration, and was given the keys. Simple. But I doubt if the friendship would stand the strain of discovering the use their future country home was put to. However, I don't suppose they will ever know." She laughed suddenly. "I am afraid there will never be peace on the domestic front again. Thérèse and Celeste have always been antagonistic, and *ma pauvre* Celeste will never recover from the fact that it was Thérèse who discovered the cassette!"

"Poor Celeste," said Sanchia.

Still laughing, Madame went out of the room. Closing the door on her, Adrian came back. "And now, no doubt, she is going to dictate tomorrow's orders!"

"She should be very fond of that little machine," said Sanchia, and then, her smile fading, she added gravely, "It saved her life."

He nodded. "I am sure you are right."

"Oh, darling," she put her hands on his shoulders, "what I can hardly believe is that we are all together again. There were times when I wondered if anything would ever go right."

"It has, and it will." He took her face between his hands, looking deeper into her eyes. "Don't you dare run any risk like that again. Can you imagine how I felt when I arrived back here and Thérèse told me where you had gone? *Mon Dieu!* When I think of that mad woman, and what might have happened—"

But she was safe and they were together, here in their own special paradise where the poison of hate and greed could no longer penetrate.

"Oh darling!" she said. "I do love you so much." And after a long moment, she added diffidently, "I wonder when on earth you began to love me—and why?"

"I began to love you when the world was young, I had been looking for you ever since then," he told her. "And at last I've got you for keeps. Yes?"

"Oh, yes—for always, please!" said Sanchia.

# HERMINA BLACK

# Fortune's Daughter

Rich, lovely Caria Barrington was used to having
anything in the world she wanted and there seemed to
be no reason why that should not include Dr. Ross
Carlton. But the last thing in the world he intended to
do was to involve himself with a pampered heiress,
until fate thrust him into her life in particularly difficult
circumstances and forced him to save her from the
consequences of her own folly.

And then there was Sonia, equally determined to
stand in Caria's way. She had her own good reasons
for making Caria pay a heavy price for that folly. She
wanted Ross herself and she was a woman who never
admitted defeat.

# Who is Lucinda?

A beautiful young woman wakens to find herself in a
London nursing home. Her head has been injured and
she is frightened to realise that she can remember
nothing of the past, not even her name. From the
papers found with her, and her solicitor's information,
she learns her identity anew. She is Lucinda Dare, an
heiress come from Canada to claim her inheritance,
victim of a train crash. Deeply puzzled, she tries to
rebuild her life from totally unfamiliar details and with
totally unfamiliar people, until a nurse remembers a
small, shabby suitcase, whose contents help to revive
the past and allow her to enjoy the romance of her
present situation.

# HERMINA BLACK

# The House in Harley Street

Fenella formed an immediate liking for Colin Bretherton
and his charming, diminutive mother, not at all the
poisonous pair his ex-wife, Aureol, depicted. He was
kind, generous, a dedicated doctor—but where Eily his
small daughter was concerned, his attitude was distant
and enigmatic. Eily's relationship to her separated
parents became the battleground for Aureol's
manoeuvres. Fenella, becoming increasingly attached to
her charge, was powerless to intervene on Eily's behalf
and found her loyalties sharply divided between the
attractive doctor and the rejected child.

# Doctor in Shadow

Every village has its own peculiar oddity, and Rothmere
in the heart of the Lake District is no exception:
Grant Vereker, the mysterious stranger, who shuts
himself away with his books, unwilling to make any
contact with the outside world.

Decima Brand has given up her nursing career to help
out her brother with the family farm, and is as
interested as anyone in Mr. Vereker. It appears that he is
a former surgeon and that he's living in some bitter
shadow of the past. To the annoyance of her admirer
Paul, Decima chips away some of the icy cool
surrounding Grant, realising that they have more than
medicine in common, but he guards his secret as
closely as ever. She determines to get to the heart of
'Doctor' Vereker, but so does Paul—for different
reasons . . .

# IRIS BROMIGE

# The Tangled Wood

Alison Blayde moves down to Sussex from London,
jobless and romantically disillusioned. But when her
Great-Uncle Arthur offers her the use of Corner Cottage
for a minimal rent and financial backing to start a small
library, it seems that all her problems have been solved.

Arthur departs the country with surprising speed,
bequeathing to Alison his feud with occupants of
Larchmere, the big house adjoining Corner Cottage. Yet
the Ridgmont family edge themselves into Alison's life in
such a way as to almost dispel the fears which had
been haunting her since Arthur had left.

Nagging doubts disallow Alison to trust her
neighbours and she is left swinging on a pendulum
between doubt and confidence—and a long, long way
from being out of the wood.

# BIG NEW EXTRA-SPECIALS FROM
# CORONET BOOKS

### Denise Robins

| | | |
|---|---|---|
| ☐ 12963 8 | LAURENCE, MY LOVE | 30p |
| ☐ 18291 1 | THE SNOW MUST RETURN | 30p |
| ☐ 02919 6 | GAY DEFEAT | 30p |
| ☐ 18300 4 | DO NOT GO MY LOVE | 30p |
| ☐ 18605 4 | ALL FOR YOU | 30p |
| ☐ 01065 7 | I SHOULD HAVE KNOWN | 30p |
| ☐ 15084 X | THE UNLIT FIRE | 30p |
| ☐ 15110 2 | SHATTER THE SKY | 30p |

### Elizabeth Goudge

| | | |
|---|---|---|
| ☐ 00855 5 | GENTIAN HILL | 40p |
| ☐ 02410 0 | THE WHITE WITCH | 45p |

### Anya Seton

| | | |
|---|---|---|
| ☐ 15701 1 | KATHERINE | 40p |
| ☐ 15693 7 | DEVIL WATER | 40p |
| ☐ 01401 6 | MY THEODOSIA | 35p |
| ☐ 15700 3 | THE TURQUOISE | 35p |
| ☐ 15699 6 | THE HEARTH AND EAGLE | 35p |
| ☐ 02713 4 | AVALON | 35p |
| ☐ 01951 4 | THE WINTHROP WOMAN | 40p |
| ☐ 02469 0 | DRAGONWYCK | 35p |
| ☐ 02488 7 | FOXFIRE | 35p |
| ☐ 15683 X | THE MISTLETOE AND SWORD | 30p |
| ☐ 17857 4 | GREEN DARKNESS | 50p |

### Jane Blackmore

| | | |
|---|---|---|
| ☐ 17877 9 | IT COULDN'T HAPPEN TO ME | 30p |
| ☐ 17878 7 | BITTER HONEY | 30p |
| ☐ 18606 2 | TWO IN SHADOW | 30p |
| ☐ 18607 0 | GIRL ALONE | 30p |

### Phyllis Whitney

| | | |
|---|---|---|
| ☐ 16856 0 | LISTEN FOR THE WHISPERER | 35p |
| ☐ 15820 4 | SEA JADE | 35p |
| ☐ 17858 2 | THE TREMBLING HILLS | 40p |

## CORONET'S NEW BESTSELLERS LIST INCLUDES:

**Hermina Black**

| | | | |
|---|---|---|---|
| ☐ | 18301 2 | DANGEROUS MASQUERADE | 30p |
| ☐ | 16079 9 | FORTUNE'S DAUGHTER | 25p |
| ☐ | 17317 3 | THEATRE SISTER AT RILEY'S | 25p |
| ☐ | 17321 1 | WHO IS LUCINDA? | 25p |
| ☐ | 17831 0 | THE HOUSE IN HARLEY STREET | 30p |

**Frances Murray**

| | | | |
|---|---|---|---|
| ☐ | 18293 8 | THE DEAR COLLEAGUE | 30p |

**Iris Bromige**

| | | | |
|---|---|---|---|
| ☐ | 18281 4 | ROSEVEAN | 30p |
| ☐ | 12947 6 | AN APRIL GIRL | 30p |
| ☐ | 02865 3 | CHALLENGE OF SPRING | 30p |
| ☐ | 15107 2 | THE TANGLED WOOD | 20p |

**Elizabeth Cadell**

| | | | |
|---|---|---|---|
| ☐ | 12797 X | THE GOLDEN COLLAR | 20p |

**Dorothy Eden**

| | | | |
|---|---|---|---|
| ☐ | 12777 5 | LAMB TO THE SLAUGHTER | 30p |
| ☐ | 18189 3 | SPEAK TO ME OF LOVE | 40p |
| ☐ | 00320 0 | THE BIRD IN THE CHIMNEY | 30p |
| ☐ | 12957 3 | SHADOW WIFE | 30p |
| ☐ | 02032 6 | SLEEP IN THE WOODS | 30p |
| ☐ | 16035 7 | VOICE OF THE DOLLS | 30p |
| ☐ | 15118 8 | BRIDE BY CANDLELIGHT | 30p |

*All these books are available at your bookshop or newsagent, or can be ordered direct from the publisher. Just tick the titles you want and fill in the form below.*

.................................................................................................................

CORONET BOOKS, P.O. Box 11, Falmouth, Cornwall.
Please send cheque or postal order. No currency, and allow the following for postage and packing:
1 book—10p, 2 books—15p, 3 books—20p, 4–5 books—25p, 6–9 books—4p per copy, 10–15 books—2½p per copy, over 30 books free within the U.K.
*Overseas*—please allow 10p for the first book and 5p per copy for each additional book.

Name ...............................................................................................................

Address ...........................................................................................................

.................................................................................................................